Re

A Dog Lady Mystery

By Ellen Carlsen

To Barbara

Ellen Carlsen Ellick

Chapter 1

In one of my dreams, I'm late for a baseball game, and I end up in the wrong neighborhood. I try to make sense of where I am because it all seems oddly but wrongly familiar. I lose my red purse and two older women offer to help me find it. I get into their car and feel something between my hip and the door. It's my purse.

"That's the way it happens sometimes, isn't it?" says one of the women.

And then I wake up, and I can't imagine why I was going to a baseball game anyway.

I wake up with four dogs on my bed in the spare bedroom in a home with someone I met a few weeks ago. Her name is Audrey Nevens. She's in her 50s or maybe early 60s, and she rescues dogs. I'm Judy Barnes. I'm 37 years old, and I've never been a dog person, but when Audrey took me in, I promised to do my part. I pitch in with the mopping, sweeping, bathing, brushing and everything else that goes along with rescuing dogs and finding them new homes.

Fortunately, I've never minded mud on my shoes. Or a little dog poo either. Most of my life (although certainly not all of it) I've known how to adapt to whatever situation life lead me into. A houseful of dogs was nothing. People once talked about me with a chuckle and lines such as "That Judy, she rolls with the punches, doesn't let anything bother her, goes with the flow, just keeps going, doesn't sweat the small stuff."

But that was when it was all pretty much small stuff. And in spite of the slogan you sometimes see, it really isn't all small stuff. My life has a before and an after. That other Judy was before. What I am now is after.

I still don't worry about dirt, poo, dog hair, chewed up shoes, muddy paw prints, ruined furniture, tattered clothes. I don't worry about anything at dog level. Replacing what they ruin is why we have thrift shops. Cleaning up after them is why we have mops, brooms, vacuums and shelves full of cleaning products. That's something I learned from Audrey, one bit of her philosophy of life and dogs.

At the foot of the bed lounges a black lab still recuperating from a gunshot wound to the upper leg. Curled into my back is a Jack Russell Terrier who'd been thrown from a car. Next to her is a Beagle, a rescue from a puppy mill. Finally, nearly pasted to my ear, is a Miniature Pinscher who came from the local animal control where she'd landed as a stray. A couple others may be on the floor next to my bed. Audrey says I may just have that special something dogs can't resist. I remind her I'm really not a dog person. I suspect most dogs are just as neurotic as we are, trying to coax love from those that don't have it to give.

After my "lost and found red purse dream", I asked Audrey what she thought about the baseball game. Is it some sort of symbol for a life well-lived? Or is life only a game? Do I want to play or just watch?

Audrey shrugged and suggested I quit trying to interpret dreams. "And don't worry about the meaning of life or anything else. It's really all about dogs."

This much I learned about Audrey quickly. She believes that if you study dogs, really study them, you'll become a better and even a happier person. But she emphasizes "better" because she says even the most despicable people can be happy. It's one of life's ironies that evil people are sometimes very happy. Their evil deeds don't bother them at all.

So forget "happy," she says. "Do right by a few dogs and you'll be just fine." I'm not there yet and I doubt I ever will be.

As I roll over and throw my legs over the side of the bed, I hear Audrey in the kitchen clattering dog dishes together. I know that sound. She's washing the dog dishes and spending more time on them than she does with our dishes. And she's whistling, something she does constantly and almost unconsciously.

The phone rings. I figure it's the first of numerous calls today from people asking Audrey to take the dogs they no longer want or can't keep for reasons that include moving, new baby, allergies, can't afford, retiring to Florida (No dogs allowed?), changing lifestyle, divorce. She calls it "dial an excuse."

I hear her laughing, so it must be one of her human friends. I'd always heard that "dog people" had trouble getting along with other humans. Good with dogs. Unskilled with fellow humans. That might be the case with some, and Audrey certainly has her set of oddities, but she seems to function fine in both worlds. Her human friends accept her as she is, so she must be doing something right.

Setting my musings aside, I dress for the day, quickly and casually in the same jeans and t-shirt I wore yesterday. Audrey is willing to give me a little time to settle in, but she still expects work from me. She expects me to get on with my life. She dishes out philosophy but very little sympathy.

Sometimes I can't even sigh this early in the day. I stumble into the kitchen and begin dishing up dog food.

Chapter 2

Six weeks earlier I'd left Missouri in a car packed with only a few remaining possessions. Everything else (and little of it) I'd put in storage. I was on a quest to learn something about my ancestors who'd settled near Redbud, Nebraska.

It had been almost a year since I'd lost my baby and then my husband. I cannot yet speak about what happened. After those unspeakable losses, I'd mastered the art of losing almost everything else that had defined my life before that day. Before that day I'd been many things – newspaper reporter, wife to a lawyer, mother to a precious infant, friend to many. I lived in a nice house in a respectable neighborhood. I had friends, clothes, shoes, hobbies, books. If someone had asked me to rank my happiness on a scale of 0 to 100, I would have picked a number over 90. My life was really that good. But that was before.

After. Well. I'd always thought tragedy would be like weights tied to my limbs and draped around my neck. I'd sink downward, bent over by despair. But instead I felt untethered, rising dangerously higher and higher, floating away. I refused to answer phone calls. I ignored bills. I sold my home. Bit by bit the remnants of what had been my life floated away too. Yes, people tried to help, but they were all so far below. I simply couldn't see them or hear what they were saying. And then the dreams started, dreams of loss and sometimes of recovery.

Eventually my life fit into the backseat of my car – one favorite painting, my e reader, two changes of clothes, a couple pair of shoes, one coat, toothpaste, my cellphone and not much else. I still had enough money to live as a vagabond for a while, so I decided to explore my family's past and leave my own past, present and the even more frightening future behind.

Every family has its stories or better put, its myths. In ours it was about my great great grandparents – Karen and Johannes, Danish immigrants who'd left their homeland to find a new life in America. I wanted to know more, to explore the family stories, some of them quite mysterious. To that end, I'd been emailing the man in Nebraska who functioned both as the local police chief and as the closest thing the community had to an historical society. Chief Sorensen. In his last email he said knew the location of my ancestor's home and had learned a few things that might interest me.

And so I left St. Louis and headed west. Interstate 64 pulled me through the suburbs and onward to Interstate 70 and beyond. What was I thinking? I called up no one to say I was leaving, I checked my reflection in the rear view mirror and barely recognized myself. I'd always been tidy about my appearance, working out three times a week to stay free of any fat, and applying makeup with an artist's touch. I'd kept my blonde hair smooth and pulled back tightly away from my face and fastened into a tidy bun. Standing only 5'2", I'd preferred heels with extra height. Clothes? Only the best and never a wrinkle. Now I saw someone with hastily combed hair barely contained in a low pony tail. Several loose hairs floated around my face. My lips seemed permanently chapped, and two thin lines snaked away from the outer corners of my pale eyes and even paler lashes. I wore a wrinkled t-shirt, shorts and flip flops. But oddly, I saw a smile, a timid smile, the smile of one who'd escaped a prison and dared wonder if she'd actually gotten away.

Four hours later I approached Kansas City and looked for the exit that would take me north. I'd visited Nebraska a few times before and knew I-29 would be straight and a little lonely. It was. Once on the highway north, the traffic thinned and I looked out over fields that stretched farther and farther away. The horizon ran from me, and I chased it. By late afternoon I finished my interstate driving and instead drifted on a rural Nebraska road. Finding Redbud was a little like finding the mythical town no one had seen for hundreds of years. One minute you're circling a city and before you know it, you're following directions that sound a lot like "straight ahead and on to nowhere. "

But by late afternoon I found Redbud and turned into a motel's parking lot outside of town. After I checked in, I walked outside for a while, noticing most of all the sky, which seemed to drop down to my knees, enclosing me in a way that seemed a little sinister. Sweat trailed down my neck, and I pulled my T-shirt away from my skin, flapping it back and forth in a futile attempt for a breeze. Summer was just as muggy here as in Missouri. Then a hot wind blew my way, twirling dust in its path. Several pieces of paper lifted from the ground and circled towards me, sticking finally to my thighs. I pulled one off and found it was a check made out to Redbud Area Dog Rescue. I decided that my first task in the morning would be to return this check to its proper place.

And that's how I began my new life. As soon as I handed over the check to Audrey, she took a close look at me and pulled me into her house. To her I must have looked like just another stray in need of rescue. I couldn't say no. I explained my desire to research my past and she nodded sagely.

"It'll take some time," she said. "You'll need a place to stay. And I can always use help."

She also knew Chief Sorensen and said she knew most of the old-timers in the area too. "I love a good mystery," she added. And then she began introducing me to the mysteries and plain realities of dog rescue.

Chapter 3

With all the dogs fed, Audrey and I begin releasing them from their kennels.

I remind her again, "I'm not really a dog person, you know." And in that moment, a dog that might be some kind of pointer bounds towards me and nearly knocks me over.

"Off Off," yells Audrey. "Don't let him do that. Turn your back on him. Don't touch him until he's on all fours or better yet, sitting."

"Off Off!" I scream. And then, "Sit!" Amazingly, the dog who is named Gage does sit, shaking with the anxiety of needing to hold the position.

"Pet him. Praise him!" Tell him he's a good boy!"

"Good boy! Good boy!" I pat him a few times and lead him and several other dogs outdoors. Audrey tosses me a tennis ball. I watch as Gage leaps over two bushes at once and begins circling the yard.

Close by my side is an older dog. I think her name is Tiffany. She sniffs my ankles and ambles about the yard. More my style. My bedmates are here too, sniffing the air and watering the grass.

Audrey steps outside with coffee cup in hand. She's a tall, slim woman with curly hair that seems to almost double the size of her head. Anytime, day or night, Audrey's hair is the same unchanging whirl of brown and grey.

Audrey surveys the nine dogs now exploring the yard with various levels of energy. Then she introduces me to one of the new dogs.

"This is Kaci. She's just a plain brown dog, but very nice." Kaci looks up as if she has something to add. She steps between the two of us and just stands there keeping us company.

"I like her. Is she always this quiet and calm? If she is, I like her." I scratch her behind her ears. "Not much to look at though, is she?"

"Shhh. Don't hurt her feelings."

This is how my days begin. I help feed dogs and supervise the early morning outdoor play. While I'm busy with what I call the "upstairs dogs," Audrey goes downstairs to the walkout basement where she keeps about eight little dogs. These have indoor and outdoor play areas separate from the dogs I'm now watching. Their numbers include a spritely Chihuahua and several timid dogs rescued from a Missouri puppy mill.

The most frightened of all is a small Cocker Spaniel named Natalie who might be the loneliest dog I've ever seen. She still stays as far away from any human as possible. She shivers if you touch her. But touching her means catching her, and that's sometimes impossible.

After early morning playtime, I clean crates, mop the floor, toss dog beds into the washing machine and finally sit down to begin going through emails --68 new messages. Some are from shelters and individuals asking Audrey to take a dog from them. A few are from people interested in adopting a dog (yeah!). A couple messages are from people who have adopted dogs and have attached joyous updates with new pictures. Unfortunately, one of today's messages is from someone wanting to know how to return the dog they'd adopted. The rest are from foster parents and other volunteers with questions and comments. Some need vet appointments. Others are having problems and want to trade for an easier dog. As I deal with each individual email, new ones continue to pop up.

After the email task (or the first email task of the day), I begin updating the website with information about which dogs will be at the weekend's adoption event. All the while, I'm glad that Audrey is the one answering the phone, which seems to ring every few minutes.

Napping dogs encircle my desk. Soon they will wake up and insist on some more outdoor play.

I move on to writing a new blog. This is another job Audrey turned over to me. I decide to write about Gigi, an opinionated Pekingese who was back with us for the second time because of her "territorial issues." I take a cute picture of her with her nose in the air and title this blog "Gigi has a High Opinion of Herself."

Perhaps we can all learn something from Gigi. She has a rather too high opinion of herself. You know the type. Nose in the air. Too good for your other friends.

That's our Gigi. She had a good home but believed that her human companion was associating with persons beneath her station. That's beneath Gigi's station to be clear. Gigi was deliriously happy as long as it was just her and her human. But let someone else come into the house and Gigi was decidedly and demonstratively unhappy.

Gigi's owner knew to keep the disapproving Gigi on a leash whenever company came by. Friends tolerated Gigi even though the little Pekingese did everything she could to let them know they were of lowly status.

Then one day one of the neighbors came into Gigi's home without knocking first. Gigi displayed her disapproval in unacceptable ways that were uncomfortable to the neighbor's left ankle. Oh dear.

Much to Gigi's initial delight, her owner's friends now refused to come by Gigi's home anymore. Unfortunately for Gigi, her owner decided she needed her friends more than she needed Gigi.

And that's why Gigi is back with us. She is trying to learn humility, and we think she will still make someone a wonderful pet.

There's a morality lesson here for all of us -- or maybe more than one. Be careful what you wish for. And try not to hold too high an opinion of yourself.

Pleased with myself and happy to be done with it, I take care of a few more emails, shut down the computer and decide to take the Jack Russell terrier and the black Labrador retriever out to the pool. I borrow one of Audrey's swimming suits, the one that almost fits me, and have what counts as a rollicking good time swimming with dogs. Unfortunately, I run into a problem bringing the two dogs back inside. Ruby the Jack Russell gets away from me. I shove Lena the lab into the house and begin shuffling down the driveway after Ruby. I'm wearing only the swimsuit that doesn't quite fit and flip flops. I have a towel tied around my waist.

I'm grateful we don't have a lot of neighbors or much traffic. There must be some law against a woman in an ill-fitting swimming suit chasing after a fit and wildly yipping Jack Russell terrier. Ruby is yipping because of her joyous discovery of two horses down the road.

"Ruby! Come now!" I scream, thinking that any minute one of the horses will kick her in the head. "Ruby!" I try to attract her attention by waving the towel that had slipped off my waist. Ruby yips madly. The horses snort rudely. Ruby leaps for one of the horse's tail. I can't look. "Ruby, Come Here Now!"

Still no response. With flip flops slapping the pavement, I hustle back home, one hand trying to keep the towel around my waist. I grab my car keys and a fist full of dog treats. And then I realize that Lena the Lab has overturned the computer table in her effort to obtain a better view of the excitement. I ignore the mess and pray that the computer still works. Then I return in the car and wave the treats at Ruby. It works. She wiggles my way for the treat in my outstretched arm. I grab her and pitch her into the car's front seat, scrambling in beside her, hoping and hoping no one was witnessing this or worse yet, taken pictures.

Somehow we all survive the day. I take dogs outside again (upstairs and downstairs), shower, and make it to the vets in time to pick up a dog that has just had eye surgery. I must look frazzled because the vet takes extra time to assure me that the eye surgery dog will be just fine. She even pats my hand a couple times. I nod and try not to mist up.

Back home, Audrey is waiting.

"Hurry," she says. "We're going to Bella's."

Chapter 4

An hour later Audrey and I push open the door of Bella's, the cozy B&B plus local diner that is the favorite gathering spot for Audrey and other Redbud residents. When it opened – something new in town!—it was big news. "Aren't we silly?" Audrey sighed, "We all got so worked up about a new place in town? It was all anyone talked about for weeks."

Audrey introduced me to the restaurant's owners – Bella and Carl, both refuges from New York City.

"Believe it or not, they got lost in Nebraska on their way to California, drifted into Redbud and saw the need here. They just then and there decided to stay. Imagine that!"

Imagine that indeed. I looked around. I loved the place. Bella and Carl had purchased a rundown old house, remodeled it into a small Bed & Breakfast (two bedrooms) with a just-the-right-size room for dining, meeting friends, reading, maybe even thinking. I noticed brick red walls, tables, sofas and chairs, an atmosphere part reading room, part restaurant, part your best friend's living room. Bella's would have been a "find" in almost any large city, especially if the food was as good as Audrey said it was. This place had to be a mirage. It couldn't possibly be real and here in Redbud, Nebraska.

"And they like me and tell me everything they hear," Audrey beamed, as she dropped into a chair in "her" corner. She loved dogs, but I already knew she had a couple other passions: the latest gossip and a good mystery. Audrey went to bed every night with a mystery novel. But a mystery in or near Redbud? That was even better.

"So, what's up?" she asks, as cold drinks and a tray of vegetables with dip appear in front of us seconds before both Bella and Carl slid into chairs across from us. Audrey's in a loose purple sundress that floats around her as she moves. Her cheeks are red, her earrings dangling, and her hair defying gravity as it twirls almost straight out from her face. I'm in the shorts, t-shirt and flip flops that started my day. My hair is, as always, pulled back loosely in a low pony tail. Bella and Carl are in matching starched khaki shorts and bright yellow short-sleeved shirts.

Bella's response is breathy and quick: "Something's happening at Old Man Schmidt's place. You know, the old guy with the puppy factory."

"Puppy mill," Carl corrects her.

"Well?" Audrey looks at Bella and then Carl. "What? And, of course I know who he is and what he is."

In spurts, Bella begins her story of how the inspector from the state Department of Agriculture had been in earlier and said he was on his way out to inspect Old Man Schmidt's. Bella described in detail what the inspector was wearing, what he ate, what he said about his family, what expression he had on his face when he talked, and almost everything he said except what he said he might do at Schmidt's place other than inspect it. Carl interrupted Bella now and then with a two or three word comment. I was already thinking of them as The Walrus and The Words. Carl, of course, is the Walrus, a square and robust man whose drooping mustache hid a mouth that could smile or frown unseen. He looked amused and thoughtful. Bella was The Words, a constant talker, always in motion. She wore her auburn hair in a stylish boyish cut. When she talked, she seemed to blow words into the air and rearrange them with her hands.

Audrey actually reached across the table and snatched Bella's hands, forcing them to the table top.

"So I'm guessing you *think* he's going to shut the place down. But you don't really know." She let go of Bella's hands, thinking she couldn't get her words out without waving her hands about.

"Well, no." Her hands floated upwards. "But I really think I felt something. It was like he wanted to tell me what he was doing, but knew it wouldn't be very professional of him."

Carl lowers his head and stares at the hands he'd folded prayer-like on the table before him. "I felt the same way."

"You too? Why?"

"Bella does have a gift for reading people." He winked at Audrey. "Or maybe the inspector was heading your way after he finished with Schmidt. Everything ship shape at Redbud Area Rescue?"

Audrey sniffed and tossed her head. "Of course. And besides, he was at my place last week. I'm good for at least a year before I need to

14

worry about another inspection. Not that I need to worry." She emphasized the last and nodded.

I decided I'd been quiet long enough. "So what exactly is a puppy mill?"

All three turned to me then as if I'd just stepped out of the mist.

"She speaks," said Carl. I'm guessing he was smiling behind his mustache. His eyes twinkled.

"So here's my puppy mill lecture," Audrey began. Puppy Mill is a derogatory term for a substandard commercial dog breeding facility. Some people call every commercial breeding facility a puppy mill, but I don't go quite that far. I reserve the term for places breeding too many dogs, too many breeds, all living in filthy condition while receiving minimal vet care. Some of the dogs live their entire lives in cages and are literally bred to death. The people who own these places care only about the money they can make from the puppies."

"Oh." I think I knew that, and I knew Redbud Area Dog Rescue had a few puppy mill dogs, but maybe I'd never really paid attention to news about dogs before.

"Some of them do a better job, and I don't call them puppy mills although I'm still unhappy about the emphasis on making money with dogs," Audrey added.

Carl looked up and challenged Audrey. "But don't you make money with Redbud Area Dog Rescue?"

Audrey nearly levitated. When she came back down, she exploded, "I most certainly don't! There's no money in rescue – not if you're doing it right and giving the dogs the care they require. That's something I've told a good many rescue wannabees who thought they might support themselves with dog rescue. If there's one thing that's worse than a puppy mill, it's a disreputable rescue, and there are some of those too." She literally huffed a few times before pointing out that she was retired with a pension and had also put away a little money thanks to a few shrewd (or lucky) investments.

"So this Old Man Schmidt is one of the bad ones?" I asked.

"Sadly, yes. He and his wife started their dog breeding business right after World War II when the government saw puppies as a solution

15

to rural poverty and encouraged rural people to raise puppies. Farmers had room and experience with livestock. The public loved purebred puppies. That was the argument, anyway, and breeding more puppies must have seemed like a good idea at the time. But many of those who decided to breed purebred dogs knew nothing about dogs or dog breeds. A lot of them didn't even like dogs. Dogs were just livestock, money makers.

Bella jumped in, hands waving about. "I've heard the Schmidt place wasn't always so bad. They started with good intentions and good hearts. People around here mainly knew them from church, so they didn't want to believe all the talk about them operating a puppy mill."

"Maybe they tried harder at first, but I'll bet he has 500 dogs now and God only knows how many puppies. And after his wife died, he tried to do most of the work himself. Now he has a couple teenagers who come in now and then, but he's well into his 80s now and should have shut down long ago." Audrey pauses to catch her breath. "Besides, there's no way he can meet the new standards. Thank God most of the puppy mill states are tightening standards for breeders, making sure the dogs have more space, exercise and vet care and that they aren't overbred. A lot of the dog breeding facilities are shutting down not just here but in other states. Missouri saw more than 1,000 shut down in two years because of the higher standards. That more than cut in half their number of commercial breeders."

"Progress," Carl pronounced. "Once in a while we do see progress in this world of ours."

"A little," murmured Audrey. "I don't suppose you want to hear me talk about dogs dying in animal shelters and the need to spay or neuter more dogs."

"Not today, but thank you anyway," said Bella, smiling widely.

We all crunched on vegetables and sipped our drinks for a while. Then Audrey looks across at Bella and Carl again.

"So that was it? That was ALL your news?"

"Well, not ALL the news," Carl winked. "We also thought you might want to hear about the woman who's been staying here for the past week. Today she let us know that she's buying a farmhouse with 17 acres and plans to open an animal shelter there."

Now Audrey sat up straight. She welcomed anyone who wanted to help dogs, but she didn't want anyone stealing away her foster homes and volunteers. And she certainly didn't want to be the last to know about someone new in the dog rescue world.

"Who? Anyone I know?"

Bella lifted one hand high, demanding attention. "I doubt it. She isn't from around here. I think she bought the place she's moving into before she even visited Redbud. I did find that a little strange. And she looks very Big City to me. I should know having been a city girl myself. Expensive clothes. Perfect hair. Beautiful nails. Well that might not describe me, but it's her for sure. I just can't see her cleaning up dog poo. But she told us we could just call her The Dog Lady. And then she laughed."

"Which place did she buy?" Audrey asked.

"You know that place with all the balconies between here and Pella? It's been on the market a while.

Now I sat up a little straighter. Is it a yellow house? Several buildings out back?

I knew exactly which place it was. Since moving in with Audrey, I'd driven out to look at that particular farmhouse five or six times. It was where my ancestors had lived.

"I wanted to buy that place."

They all stared at me. Then Audrey smiled.

"I guess we'll be visiting there soon and introducing ourselves to this new Dog Lady. I don't mind giving up the title. I'd rather think of myself as something more than just The Dog Lady, anyway.

Bella's hands went up as she remembered something more. "Oh, and she had someone with her when she checked out – another woman who also didn't look like she spent much time around dogs. The other woman came in the door just as the, ahem, Dog Lady checked out. They seemed surprised to see each other and not in a good way. But they walked out together and talked for a bit just outside the door. They seemed friendlier then. Then they left together with one car following the other."

"Do you remember their names?" I asked. Bella didn't hesitate. "Our visitor had one of the Scandinavian names ending in "sen" or "son." Carlsen? No Harrison. Yes, that's it. Harrison. And I definitely remember the other woman's name because it sounded so phony. She introduced herself as Goldie La Chien."

Audrey stood up so fast her chair fell backwards. A line appeared between her eyes, and she frowned. Then she picked up her chair and sat back down. She paused a moment before speaking again, then looked up with a smile.

"A genuine Redbud mystery. Add that to the day's other mystery."

"Another mystery?" We all asked at once.

"Not in Redbud, but I spent part of my day calling other rescue friends. I've been trying to reach a rescue friend in Topeka, Kansas, -- Michelle Ames. She's not answering phones or emails. I wouldn't have been concerned, but she's usually so quick to get back with me. "

"And?"

"I'm waiting for a call. We decided to ask the local police to check on her." She shrugged. "She's probably fine and she'll be furious with me for doing this. But…." And again she shrugged. "What else could I do? " She smiled. "She'll learn to return my calls."

We all looked at her without speaking.

Then Audrey broke the silence. "While I wait, what's for dinner?"

Chapter 5

We returned home from Bella's and waited for a call from Topeka. Audrey poured us both a glass of wine. Audrey is predictable and consistent when it comes to beverages. She drinks three cups of coffee every morning and likes a glass or two of wine several nights a week. Never more than three cups of coffee and never more than two glasses of wine. The rest of the time, she drinks bottled water.

While we sipped our wine and waited for a call, I kept busy with a blog for next week. Since I'd just learned more about puppy mills, I decided my next blog would be about Natalie. I titled it "Natalie All Alone."

Natalie is a small cocker spaniel, a damaged soul who only wants to be alone. The one picture I caught of her in the back yard shows a frightened, lonely dog surrounded by emptiness. She is all alone in the world. This little puppy mill dog refuses to accept me as a friend.

Natalie came to us after her breeder went out of business and sold or gave away all his dogs. This breeder needed to go out of business. His exodus is good news. He was not a good breeder. He was a puppy miller.

Before Natalie came to us, no one ever petted, held or even talked kindly to her. No one ever called her a good dog. She must have lived forever inside her cage with only occasional contact with a rough handler.

And what will we do with Natalie? Although I haven't given up, I fear Natalie may be beyond help. On the few times she's been free in the back yard, no one has been able to catch her -- even with a leash trailing behind her. She only wants to get as far away as possible at as fast a speed as she can manage. To coax her inside, we leave a door propped open, turn out the lights and pretend we're not there. Finally, she sneaks in on her own and hides in a dog crate.

Once a day, I gently pull her from her hiding place and lift her onto the sofa next to me. I pet her. Usually she shivers, afraid to move. But occasionally she relaxes and even sneaks a look at me. That's all I can report in the way of progress.

She's now taking two anti-anxiety drugs, and I'm hoping she'll calm down enough so that we can begin to socialize her in earnest. But for now, she is still Natalie All Alone.

Finally, the phone rang. The news was bad.

Chapter 6

The Killer

Killing the Topeka Dog Lady was easier and more fun than I'd expected.

I hate dogs and it only makes sense that I would hate Dog Ladies, those crazy women who think they are saving the world whenever they save a dog and find it a new home. Some men rescue dogs, but no one ever calls them Dog Gentlemen, now do they?

But why kill Dog Ladies? Or Dog Gentlemen (tee hee). Ask Audrey. My beef is with her, and this is just one way to let her know that I'm out here and I'm after her. She'll get the message.

So I walked up to the door and put on my best smile. When I finished my little speech, the Topeka Dog Lady followed me out to my car to see what I'd brought her. After that it was easy. She trusted me. We chatted away about dogs, and I did a wonderful job if I do say so of sounding like just another dog lover.

It was so easy. She was so trusting. She was so nice to put all her dogs away in their kennels so we could get acquainted without distraction. I knew the exact moment she realized I was not a friend. In her eyes. Her mouth dropped open. She tried to get to her feet.

I left her where she fell and walked away from the rising cacophony of hysterical dogs.

Chapter 7

We didn't meet the new dog lady or dog ladies (whichever the case) the next day and by the end of the week we still hadn't made it out to the farmhouse of my ancestors. After the Topeka police called Audrey with the news that Michelle was dead, Audrey spent a lot of time trying to find out the details – but without much success. They weren't yet sure if the death was an accident, suicide or murder.

Huh. What does that mean? They don't know? But what killed her? Their answers were vague. Investigation underway. A story in the Topeka newspaper only said that she was found dead and the cause was still unknown. The rest of the article outlined her work in dog rescue.

Then Audrey spent most of the next morning making sure that the dogs at Michelle's place were being transferred to other rescue. She offered to take any leftovers that could be transported to Nebraska. She talked with other dog rescuers across the country who knew Michelle. She emailed everyone on her list that might know Michelle.

Then the next day the Agriculture Department inspector called Audrey to see if she'd take some of Old Man Schmidt's dogs. Bella was right. The state was shutting down this puppy mill. The inspector contacted several humane societies and rescue groups, and over the next few days, vans arrived from several states, all to help some sad dogs who deserved better and now would have a chance to be pets. Audrey called in her volunteers and lined up foster homes for as many dogs as possible.

I didn't know what to expect. I didn't yet even think of myself as a dog person. But when I saw the pathetic animals crowded together in cages carpeted with feces, I felt something slip inside me. Audrey pulled several dogs out of a cage, and handed one of them to me. I found myself trying to find the face inside a tangled rug of fur. If I'd seen it on the ground, I would not have identified it as an animal.

Audrey saw me hesitate. "Don't worry. We'll take this batch off to grooming right away....and then to the vet clinic. They look tragic, but this is their lucky day."

I wasn't so sure. .I kept thinking of Natalie and wondered how many of these dogs were too damaged to ever recover. Audrey must have read my thoughts.

"Most of these mill dogs are resilient. They come around as soon as they realize they are safe. They wake up to a new life. It's one of the most heartening things you'll ever see. And you will see it."

But I was tired of tragedy and wondered if anyone ever did survive. My mind lifted away and I worked without thinking, handing dogs off to Audrey's volunteers or to dog crates in her van. And then I helped load other dogs into the buses that had arrived from a couple of the larger humane societies.

The inspector shouted instructions, pointed from kennel to kennel and marked up all the needed paperwork. Old Man Schmidt stayed in his house. We never saw him.

When we left for home, I held in my lap my first rescued dog – the matted rug. I named her Faith and stayed with her later at the groomers, watching a 6 pound dog emerge. The groomer shaved off the fur as if peeling an apple. Faith's matted coat fell to the floor in long strips. Finally she could move freely and see ahead of her. In the weeks ahead, Faith and the others we took into Redbud Area Dog Rescue would see the vet and receive all the care they needed. They would all be spayed or neutered, vaccinated, and given dental care. Some would lose most or even all of their infected teeth.

Chapter 8

I dreamed I'd lost a contact lens. I was playing basketball when someone elbowed me and I lost my right contact. I dropped to my knees and felt all over for it. By the time I found it, the lens had quadrupled in size and no longer fit my eye. All the other players starred at me. One of them said, "Are we playing or not?"

I don't play basketball. I don't even wear contact lenses. I hate these dreams, and I take Audrey's advice and try not to interpret this one either. Too easy, I think. These dreams seem to take me backwards, and I'd rather draw a curtain to shut away my past. I know there are those who say you should talk everything out and explode your emotions outward like some gigantic sneeze. They're wrong. I think they're wrong. But even if I wanted to talk it out, I'm pretty sure my voice would disappear.

I don't want to relive my past and my pain. But I'm drawn to the past of my ancestors.

I'd finally arranged to meet with Chief Sorensen, who was also the town historian. And I hoped also to drop in on the new dog lady in the home where my ancestors once lived. After hurrying through my morning chores – the feeding, the playing, the emails and all, I excused myself and snatched my car keys.

Even before I knocked on his door, I heard conversation inside. One voice pleading, the other soothing.

"Please be still. Please. Someone is at the door and I need you to be quiet for a while."

"Harrumph. Always telling me to shut up. I'm tired of being quiet."

And then the door swung open and a tall balding man stuck his head out and smiled. He had that pleasant Midwestern look about him and misty blue eyes. One thing he didn't look like to me was a police chief. I would have guessed high school principal.

"Come in. Come in. You must be Judy."

I stepped into a living room that also didn't look like a police chief's home. I saw dainty doilies on the arms of the sofa and colorful throws draped over the back of the sofa and several chairs. In a rocker in one corner slumped one of the oldest men I'd ever seen. Although it was August, a knitted blanket covered his legs and left his feet exposed, showing off hand-knitted socks. His head seemed too small, almost shriveled.

"I'm 110 years old, and I leak from all my orifices," croaked the old man. "And my grandson leaves me alone too much."

"Dad. Be nice, please," Chief Sorensen said. "This is Judy. Her great great grandparents lived in the country near here in the 1870s and beyond. She's trying to solve a few family mysteries. And Judy, this is my grandfather, Lars Sorensen."

I smiled and nodded in the old man's direction. "What a lovely lap blanket," I said.

"Harrumph," he replied, and added, "Maybe I knew your people."

"Karen and Johannes Jensen. Might you have heard of them?"

The old man stared at me as Chief Sorensen nudged me towards a room off to the left of the living room. He whispered a little too close to my ear. "He'll say he knew them. He claims to know everyone."

As the door clicked shut, I heard the old man, whose hearing must still be pretty good, mumbling "I do know everyone. He just doesn't believe me."

"You'll have to excuse my father. He's really a fine man and he raised me after my parents died in an auto accident. But he's 110 years old this month and very frustrated with all the limitations of old age, so he can be difficult at times. But there's nothing wrong with his mind. Sharp as ever."

"I understand," I replied, appropriately, I thought, although I'd never known any centenarians and could only imagine the frustration that went with advanced age. "How long has he lived with you?"

The Chief rubbed a hand across his balding scalp. "Actually, I live with him. This was his place and mine as I was growing up. I moved back here 15 years ago to help him and, I might add, to help myself as well. By then, I was ready to retire from my life as a big city detective. Tired of the city. Tired of the life I was living. Redbud welcomed me and I haven't regretted the move.

"But how do you manage? It must be a lot of work."

"I have a nurse who comes in once a day – sometimes more often if I'm especially busy."

Audrey had filled me in on Chief Sorensen, so I already knew most of his story. He'd grown up in Redbud, moved away to join a Chicago police force, advanced to detective level and saw too much of murder and messed-up lives. He'd lost his wife to divorce long ago; a daughter lived in California and visited once a year, if that. Redbud had welcomed him and his expertise, but Audrey wondered if he didn't at least occasionally miss some of the Chicago action.

"I don't miss the city at all," he said, interrupting my thoughts. "Redbud keeps me busy, and I have four fine young officers to supervise. And not that much crime although small towns can still have problems. But here in Redbud, I feel like my actions can keep people safe. This is my town, and I'll do what it takes to take care of it."

Finishing his little speech (probably one he gave all the time), he took a seat at a long table in the room he'd converted to an office for his historian and genealogical activities. File cabinets lined all the walls, and he had several piles of file folders on the table.

"And all of this (he spread his arms wide) keeps me busy too. I majored in history in college, so this is a natural fit."

I guessed Chief Sorensen to be a fit 50ish man –maybe even late '50s. He was broad-shouldered and almost too thin. Four horizontal lines creased his forehead, and his intense blue eyes locked on mine as I took a seat across from him. Maybe high school principals and police chiefs look alike.

"You said you'd found out a few things that might be helpful, Chief Sorensen."

"Please, call me Randy. I'm wearing my historian hat now."

"Randy."

"I found a few things. " He explained that he'd found records showing that Johannes Jensen had purchased railroad land in 1875 and purchased some additional land a few years later. Railroad land was

26

better located that the free land that went to homesteaders. "So he started out with at least enough money to set himself up better. The original land cost him $550 which was actually quite a bit then."

Then he spread out another document. "This is his will."

This was new. I hadn't known about a will.

"It shows a couple interesting things. He left more than $30,000 when he died in 1912. Today that would be equivalent to almost half a million, quite a bit for a simple farmer to leave behind. And that was before the farm was sold. Each of his children inherited enough to buy a very nice house. A couple of these homes are in town, still occupied, and still fine structures. You'll probably want to see them. As for the farm, the property was divided up and sold. The house there has been remodeled several times, but I think part of it is the original home of your ancestors."

"I'll want to visit the house," I added. I'm planning to go there next."

"Oh?" He put both hands flat on the table. "I've been thinking about the lady who moved in there. I should get out there myself soon. In a town the size of Redbud, it's important to know why a mystery woman from an East Coast city is moving into an old farm house in Nebraska."

"And planning to start her own dog rescue group...."I started to add.

He laughed. Almost a hoot. I'm betting our friends at the B&B told Audrey that just to see how she would react."

"But she said she wanted to be known as The Dog Lady."

"I think Audrey has that title nailed down around here."

We talked a little more and then we decided what to do next. While I visited the new Dog Lady (and maybe the mysterious Goldie La Chien as well), he was going to look through newspapers and correspondence to look for more clues about my ancestors.

"The money Johannes left when he died was significant for the time," the Chief said, "but I'm not sure it reaches the level of the kind of fortune your family's stories suggest. We may need to dig a little deeper." And then he winked.

27

As I stepped out, I looked at the old man, Chief Sorensen's grandfather. He was staring at the screen on a laptop computer which must have been next to him all along. I said good-by, but he never looked up. He was intensely involved in an online card game.

Chapter 9

As I drove out to meet the new Dog Lady and snoop around the home of my ancestors, I wondered what Chief Sorensen knew about me. If he needs to know about all the newcomers and strangers in town, he might have checked me out a bit. What could be more suspicious than someone just showing up one day with only a few possessions and landing in the home of a woman who rescued dogs?

I also wished I'd asked him about Bella and Carl. I'm betting he checked them out when they drifted in and decided to stay.

He must know a lot of secrets, I thought. I, for one, wanted to keep my secrets to myself. I suspect most people feel that way.

The countryside near Redbud is an area of rolling hills. This is not yet the Great Plains where early settlers lived in sod homes surrounded by flat, tree-less plains; instead, these Eastern Nebraska settlers like my ancestors lived in houses built from the wood they harvested from trees that grew near the Missouri River. As I topped one hill, I saw ahead of me my destination. I reached in my purse with one hand to pull out a picture of a square two-story farm home, a picture that had been my grandmother's.

I pulled up in front of a two-story yellow house that looked something like the picture I now held in my hand. The house was set far in from the road and the only other house visible was across the road and also set far back. I felt the emptiness and the silence. I thought of *Natalie All Alone* and wondered if that frightened cocker spaniel saw the world this way.

I was half way to the house when I noticed the front door was open, waving an unhappy welcome or maybe a warning. I stopped, feeling phantom fingers trailing up my spine. For a couple seconds, I thought of bolting for my car and rocketing away. But instead I moved on, calling out what I thought was a friendly, "Hello, anyone home? Hello?"

No one responded.

I crept closer. "Hello? Anyone home?" No dog barked. What kind of Dog Lady was she? No dog. All silence.

I held my breath and listened, waiting for a sound, any sound. I imagined for a moment a step creaking under someone's foot, then a shadow drifting past a window. Did I sense a soft cough? Someone exhaling?

But no. All I heard was the call of a single bird. I exhaled and stepped to the door.

I've read plenty of murder mysteries. I've listened to lawyers discuss crimes and their consequences. I was braced for the possibility that I might walk into something unpleasant. And yet when I saw the body stretched out just inside the door, one arm stretched forward, my initial response was to reach for her hand, thinking she just needed help getting to her feet. My fingers stopped just short of hers as reality took over. I straightened up and stepped back. Then I leaned forward again and rested my hand against her neck, checking for a pulse. Nothing. No pulse. But also no blood. No signs of violence. Just a smartly dressed woman face down on the floor. Her slim white pants clean and pressed, her tan blouse tied at her waist, sun-shaped gold earrings shining. This was certainly not the way for a Dog Lady to dress. But then this Dog Lady didn't seem to own any dogs anyway. And even Dog Ladies dress up now and then. Maybe. But in the country? During the day? When home alone? I lifted my eyes to the room beyond the body and saw a small table with the remains of a wine bottle and empty glasses. A crisp yellow tablecloth seemed almost to reflect the light from the window. I was about to step over the body and advance on to the table when I realized I needed to do something. One just doesn't find a dead body and proceed to snoop through the house.

Then oh my God it really hit me. A dead body. I've just stumbled over a dead body. This is worse than a murdered Dog Lady in Topeka. This is a dead Dog Lady or maybe a dead faux Dog Lady right here in Redbud. Was there a connection? What should I do?

I stepped back outside and tugged my cellphone from my purse and poked around for the card with Chief Sorensen's number. Within minutes of making my call, I heard the distant wail of a siren and soon a young, uniformed officer jogged in my direction. He introduced himself as Kevin and peeked around me through the open door.

30

He looked like he'd just graduated from high school last week, but he proceeding to take my statement while staying clear of the body. As he took down my words, he kept asking if I needed to sit down or if he could offer me something to drink. As I answered his questions about what I'd seen and why I was there, I heard my voice shaking. This seemed odd because I didn't think I was upset at all. I thought I was handling this well. But I couldn't stop the vibration in my vocal cords.

Then I noticed that his voice was shaking a little bit too.

"Actually, this is my first dead body. I've only been on the force a couple months," he said.

"But it's certainly not my first," said Chief Sorensen, who had stepped silently up behind us. Kevin and I both turned in surprise. We hadn't heard him pull up.

The Chief took over and I watched. "It might be natural causes," he said, noting the obvious lack of blood or evidence of violence. "But I doubt it. Something doesn't say natural causes to me."

I don't know what caused his doubt, but he immediately made another call which would soon brought crime scene technicians and other detectives from the county police. I hung around long enough to see the yellow tape pulled into place, the booties slipped over shoes, the removal of a laptop computer and wine glasses in plastic bags. Chief Sorensen and a couple others walked around the house, pointing here and there, heads bowed as they walked side by side. At one point Chief Sorensen came back to me where I was now sitting in my car with the door open, wiping sweat from my forehead.

"Are you sure you've never met her before?"

"Never"

"And she doesn't look at all familiar?"

"I've never seen her."

"Does she know anyone in town?"

"She knows Bella and Carl. She stayed there. Unless the dead woman is the one who called herself Goldie La Chien." I told her about the woman who had arrived as the first woman was checking out of Bella's.

"Has Audrey been here yet?"

I didn't know.

31

Chief Sorensen told me I was free to leave, but I stammered a bit about wanting to tour the home of my ancestors and walk about the property

"Not now. Not now. This is not the time," he interrupted.

I agreed, reluctantly, and started up my car. But before I pulled out on the road, I called Audrey. "Can you meet me at Bella's?"

"I'm pretty busy now. What's up?"

"There's been another murder. Right here in Redbud." Was I being overly dramatic? What if it was just natural causes?

Chapter 10

I sprinted from my car to Bella's front door but stopped suddenly as I saw through the window that Audrey was already there. She was engaged in animated conversation with Carl and Bella, who were again dressed in matching shorts and shirts. I saw Bella's hands in the air, Carl's head lowered like a bull preparing to charge, Audrey lifting herself from her chair to snatch Bella's hands and pull them back to earth. They all appeared to be talking at once, or in Carl's case, muttering. As I pushed open the door, I was sure I heard Audrey's voice demanding silence.

And silent was the room when I walked in and looked in their direction. All three turned their heads towards me and said nothing until I asked, "Audrey, how did you get here before me?" I'd guessed she would trail me by at least 15 minutes and more if dogs didn't all quickly return to their kennels and if she had any trouble finding her purse and car keys, a common occurrence.

Audrey just smiled. "Actually I was already in town when you called. So we've been waiting for you." Then she looked at Bella and Carl with a look I knew well. It was "the mother look," or "the teacher look." the "you-had-better-behave look." Both Carl and Bella said, almost in unison, "That's right. We've been waiting for you."

"Well?" asked Audrey, looking up at me. And then quickly, as if she just noticed the distress etched on my face, "Oh for heaven's sake, sit down. You must be a mess." She stepped towards me and put an arm around my shoulders, helped me towards a vacant chair at their table. Bella, some water for Judy, please. She looks like she's about to faint." Audrey settled me into the chair and cleared several folders off the table to make room for my drink. "And take your record-keeping with you." She waved the folders at Bella, who snatched them from Audrey, tucked them under one arm, and carried them away. When she returned with my ice water, the folders were gone.

"Tell us what happened," Audrey said, leaning towards me.

"What did you see?" added Carl.

Bella's hands fidgeted and started to rise. "Was she already dead when you got there?"

"Oh she was quite dead," I answered, and went on to describe the waving door, the body stretched out just inside the house, the wine bottle and glasses, the yellow table cloth, the arrival of the officer and then of Chief Sorensen and the other investigators.

"How did they know she was murdered?" Audrey almost whispered her question.

"I don't know, really. I didn't see any blood or any sign of struggle. The only thing that didn't seem right was that she was dressed so nicely in the middle of the day."

"Well, not to be too obvious, it looks like she'd had some company. Otherwise, why the glasses for wine. She was entertaining someone," Carl mused.

"Maybe it was the other woman I saw her with," said Bella. "Or maybe the other woman was the dead body. Oh dear."

"Of course. Of course. But when did she die? Last night? This morning? Maybe even shortly before you got there." Audrey was now in prime murder mystery mode. And I'll admit I had my mystery solving hat on too.

"And who is she? I told Chief Sorensen what I knew which wasn't much. I'd just gone out there to meet her and maybe look around the house and property a little. I wanted to see where my ancestors had lived and I was even going to encourage her to help with your dog rescue activities, Audrey. But you know what was really odd?"

"What?" I swear they all spoke at once.

"She did not have a single dog. Or cat. Or animal of any kind. She did not look at all like someone who might set up a new dog rescue group. And she didn't look like someone who'd want to be known as The Dog Lady."

"I'll second that," said Carl. "I didn't see her as a dog person at all. Way too tidy."

"Hey! Does that mean you think of me as untidy, mister!?" Audrey huffed a bit. She's good at that.

"This isn't the time for humor, Audrey." This time Carl almost growled.

I wondered. Were these friends having a little falling out? And was it because of the murder?

"It was Chief Sorensen who didn't think she died of natural causes. He was thinking murder even before the other investigators arrived. Officially, the cause is still unknown, so maybe it'll turn out not to be murder. Anyway, I told Chief Sorensen that you might know something more since you'd seen both women." Both Carl and Bella nodded.

It was then a bell jangled, alerting us to the entry of Chief Sorensen.

"Ah, just the people I need," he said. He nodded at me and said, "You might as well just head on home. I'm sure this has been a rough day."

Driving home, I almost ran off the road when I remembered something important.

I'd called Audrey to meet me at Bella's. When she asked why, I said there'd been a murder.

I hadn't said anything about who had been murdered.

Chapter 11

I dreamed about a friend from years past. We'd met at work and had kept in touch after she left the newspaper to try her luck as a freelancer. We'd meet for lunch or dinner every month or so. I'd been trying to reach her for a couple of weeks when I learned that she'd died suddenly and alone of a ruptured aneurism in the brain. I'd lost a friend. In my dream, she walked up to me as if she'd just been out of the country on vacation. I asked where she'd been. I apologized that we'd all believed she was dead. Her condo had been sold, her savings distributed to her heirs, all her clothes, paintings and other property sold or given away. I was so sorry about all that and so happy to see her. But I was mad at her too. Why hadn't she let me know where she was? She laughed and said, "Well that's just the way it happens sometimes, isn't it?"

In the three days after I discovered the dead body, Redbud Area Dog Rescue adopted out more than 10 dogs. Several people drove up from Kansas City specifically to adopt dogs they'd admired on our website: a Pekingese, a border collie, and an elderly Black Labrador Retriever. A few more dogs found their new homes at an adoption event in Omaha. I watched Tiffany and Kaci and Lena meet their new guardians. Even Ruby the Jack Russell found a home with people who couldn't imagine life without a Jack Russell. They called the next morning, worried that Ruby "wasn't active enough. Was she active with you?"

"Oh yes."

And soon she was active enough.

Gage the pointer mix who leaped over bushes found a home with a retired couple who loved pointers and lived on a lake. I told everyone around me that I wished they'd adopted me. The beagle and the miniature pinscher found homes, and so did Natalie the terrified cocker spaniel. I learned later that Natalie was attending classes for shy dogs.

Even Gigi the opinionated Pekingese found a new home, although I hold my breath waiting for a call saying she's misbehaving again.

The dogs from Old Man Schmidt's puppy mill gradually grew more confident and would all soon be ready for adoption. Faith, the little Maltese, still didn't understand why it wasn't ok to pee or poo inside, but she earned some forgiveness from me because she so quickly decided I was the most wonderful human alive. She yipped, ran in circles and leapt joyfully at my legs whenever I came near. Her ecstatic and demanding display would continue until I lifted her into my arms and rubbed noses.

I'm not a dog person yet, but I'm beginning to accept them and enjoy their company and even the work they force upon me.

The dog rescue world is a world of second chances and sometimes third and fourth. Lost, abandoned and abused dogs find homes with good people who will love and spoil them. Audrey admits that for all our successes, we must also admit to a few failures. "We're not perfect and neither are the people who adopt our dogs. But most of the time, our dogs move on to better lives." She scratches the head of one plain black dog. "Dogs are so much in the moment that once they see kindness around them, they think this is the way it has always been and always will be."

I'd like to believe in second chances. And thirds and fourths.

Aware that we had some room for more dogs, Audrey and I visited one of the rural shelters and looked over the dogs on death row, which was basically all of them. The shelter we visited was "open intake," accepting all dogs brought to it. With only so much space, the shelter regularly reached its limits and some dogs were euthanized. Some would describe such places as "kill" shelters.

Redbud Area Dog Rescue is a "no kill" shelter. But others might describe us as "closed intake." We only take in new dogs when we have room. When we don't have room, we say "no." We can add room by either finding homes for the dogs we have or finding new foster homes. This day, due to several adoptions, we had room. Audrey and I walked down the aisle between the kennels with the medium and large dogs. Their barking rattled throughout the room and beyond. Some jumped and wagged as we approached. A few backed away. We picked a yellow lab mix, a beagle, a fluffy mixed breed that might have been some kind of sheepdog, and a sleek, spotted youngster that was shaped like a Whippet.

37

I tried not to look at those we left behind, but I felt their eyes following us. We moved into the room with small dogs. We saw only three dogs there and took them all – two Chihuahuas and a heavily matted Shih Tzu.

When you can forget about those you leave behind, rescues like this feel good. We're giving some homeless dogs another chance for the good life. Life for dogs as for humans can change at any given moment. This knowledge is what gives us hope and scares us speechless. That moment when everything changes.

Today we changed the future for several dogs who were days or even just hours away from being put to sleep. As Audrey drove the van full of dogs home, I called for grooming and vet appointments. And we dreamed up names for all of them. Homer for the beagle, Sunshine for the yellow lab mix, Freckles for the spotted dog, Delilah for the sheepdog, Pablo and Picasso for the Chihuahuas, and Heidi for the Shih Tzu.

And yes, I brought up the murder. The only thing we knew for sure now was that the victim was most likely Lydia Harrison, the woman who had spent a few days at Bella's. Police had found a driver's license and other items identifying her. Fingerprints would likely further confirm her identity. The local newspaper had carried only a paragraph about a woman found dead in her home. The article said she had recently moved here from New York City. Nothing was said about murder.

What do you think happened to the other woman? The one who called herself Goldie La Chien," I asked Audrey.

"Police will certainly want to find her, I'm sure. She's either another victim or she knows what happened there." Audrey seemed reluctant to speculate more. I wondered if she had suspicions she wasn't willing to share.

"Does the name Goldie La Chien mean anything to you? Could it have been a message to someone?"

Audrey remained silent. Instead she patted the curls on one side of her heads, shrugging as the curls sprang horizontally back into their original position as soon as she lifted her hand. I couldn't believe her reaction. Miss I Love a Mystery was acting as if murder in her neighborhood was boring. What was going on here?

So I asked. "Shouldn't you be a little more excited about a murder in your hometown?"

"Redbud isn't my home town. It's my home today and maybe for the rest of my life, but I was born and raised in California. I've only lived here about eight years."

That was news to me. Was everyone here a transplant? "I thought Redbud was the kind of town where everyone was a native – or almost everyone."

Audrey seemed to be thinking. "Well, Chief Sorensen is pretty much native. He grew up here, but he spent most of his life in Chicago. She named a few of our foster parents and volunteers who had lived their entire lives in Redbud.

So it seemed Redbud was a place people left and sometimes returned to or stumbled into. All very strange, and I was now a part of the strangeness.

And why was it so easy for Audrey to guess who'd been murdered? I asked her about that, pointing out that when I'd called her I'd only mentioned murder and not the victim.

She looked at me, surprised by the question.

I saw her collecting her thoughts before she answered. That made me even more suspicious.

"I knew you were planning to see Chief Sorensen and then go meet the new so-called Dog Lady. So I figured it had to be one of those two. I put my money on the Dog Lady."

Well maybe, I thought. But her answer really didn't satisfy me. I pointed out that we still didn't know much about the murder victim except that she was from New York and had stayed at Bella's for a few days. Audrey knew something she didn't want me to know. I was sure of that. But what? And why? Maybe she just wasn't ready to trust me. And maybe I shouldn't trust her. But all things considered, I needed to trust her. She was my savior, my lifeline, my anchor. And more and more, she was now my friend.

We arrived back home and began settling in the new dogs. A few had foster parents already waiting on our front porch. Others would stay with us.

39

Each dog came complete with an overdose of shelter perfume, something we would try to replace quickly with something more pleasing.

As we worked, I thought of several things I needed to do.

I needed to write down everything I knew about my ancestors, everything my mother and grandmother had told me.

I needed to call Chief Sorensen and see if I could pry some information from him about the murder. I had a ready excuse for calling him: my genealogical research.

And I needed to let someone in St. Louis know I was still alive before I became someone else's strange dream.

Chapter 12

I was feeling bad about leaving St. Louis without notifying anyone when I realized that everyone who might care about me had my cellphone number, and I still had my cellphone and the same email address. No one had called. No one had emailed. No one. I checked my call history to see if I'd missed any calls. No missed calls. No emails lost in the spam folder. No one was worried about me. No one had reported me missing. I had really outrun my past.

With sudden clarity, I realized that my entire life was now right here in Nebraska with homeless dogs and people who loved them, a few mysterious transplants, long-dead ancestors, a murder victim and a police chief who solved murders and mysteries past and present. I had not escaped all danger or future misfortune. I had not stopped having strange dreams about losing things although the dreams scared me less now and sometimes even amused me. But my work with the dogs exhausted my body and my quest to solve the mysteries of my ancestors filled my mind, clouding over my saddest memories. My feet were not yet firmly on the ground, but I floated a little lower now.

Whenever I could, I carried Faith the little dog I'd taken home the day the state closed down Old Man Schmidt's puppy mill. I'd stroke her shaved-down coat as I whistled soft tunes and told her how beautiful she'd be one day. "We all love you, Faith," I'd reassure her. Now and then I'd catch her peeking at my face. She was now one of the dogs who slept on my bed at night, burrowing under the covers to settle somewhere near my knees.

My days still involved mopping, cleaning dog crates, feeding and exercising dogs, writing blogs, updating the rescue website, sometimes taking dogs for swims as the sticky summer days continued, shuttling dogs to vet and grooming appointments, transporting dogs to adoption events, picking up dogs from shelters, and more.

But I still found some time for other things. And I was dying (bad word) to learn more about the murder and to dig deeper into my family history. I needed an excuse to call Chief Sorensen, so I wrote down an assortment of things I'd learned from my mother and grandmother and a few things I'd learned on my own.

My grandmother had always claimed that Karen was disinherited for "marrying beneath her station." She'd been married in Denmark, but no one knew what happened to that first husband. Karen had come to America as a governess for a wealthy family and had soon met and married Johannes. She'd given birth to 11 children, including two born in Denmark. Only seven survived to adulthood. Karen, Johannes and their children enjoyed several card games but always drew the drapes when they played so others wouldn't know what they were doing. "They were good too," my grandmother told me.

Another thing my grandmother told me was that the Queen of Denmark once visited Nebraska and met with several immigrants, including my great great grandmother. This led to wistful speculation that someone in the family might be related to royalty.

What they passed on to me was a fistful of often unrelated details that told a story, but was it the real story? And let's not forget the repeated references to wealth apparently lost. But isn't that a common myth? Once upon a time we were special. Once upon a time we were rich. Then something happened. We lost it all. We've been searching for what we lost ever since.

Wanting to learn more, I'd started my own search a decade or so ago, visiting libraries and online genealogy sites. I looked through immigration and census records, baptismal reports, old newspapers, and any other records I could find. I learned a few things my mother and grandmother hadn't known or at least hadn't shared with me. One of my more interesting discoveries was that my great great grandmother Karen was not married when she gave birth in Denmark to my great grandmother. Later she married a shoemaker and had a second child. I couldn't find out what happened to that first husband. But I did find out that when Karen immigrated to America, she left her two children (then 3 and 1) behind with her brother. They joined her in Nebraska after she married Johannes.

If I closed my eyes and filled in the gaps with my imagination, my family story expanded into something richer, full of drama, shame, love, courage, renewal, loss, gain, struggle, and more.

But I wanted to learn more. Something pulled me to this place and wouldn't let me leave.

Chapter 13

The next morning I awoke from a dream in which I'd lost the cord to my laptop. I looked everywhere but couldn't find it. As I shook off the dream world, I was relieved that I could stop searching. I told Audrey about the dream and that in this dream I didn't find the lost object. Again, Audrey reminded me that dream interpretation was for fools. I should only worry about dogs.

Hah, I thought, as I carried Faith outdoors in hopes she would learn appropriate bathroom habits. Although I was free from searching for the lost cord of my dream, this day would be all about searching for answers. Chief Sorensen had said I could drop by his home later that afternoon. I hurried through my chores, exercising dogs, cleaning crates, mopping floors, answering emails, updating websites, and even swimming with a lab. Audrey spent much of her day answering phone calls and organizing her files. She still ignored my questions about the murder, saying she was "thinking it through," whatever that meant.

I know Audrey reads murder mysteries endlessly and considers herself a clever problem solver. Maybe she would suddenly figure out all the whodunit and why without any help from anyone. Or maybe she already knew. That thought crossed my mind.

I pulled up to Chief Sorensen's house just before 4 and met not Chief Sorensen but his grandfather at the door. After ringing the bell, I waited while the old man shuffled to the door pushing his walker ahead of him. He poked his head in my direction like a turtle stretching his head from his shell. Behind him, I saw the late afternoon sun casting a beam of light with dust particles floating within.

"Come in. Come it," he croaked. "My grandson is on his way." He turned and shuffled back to his chair, eased himself into it and pulled his laptop towards him. "I'm playing Faro, best card came for gamblers there is."

"I thought you were playing poker."

"Nah. Poker is for fools. Faro's the game. I played it as a young man, learned from some of the old-timers. It was the most popular game in the Old West. Lot of people don't know that.

Hunched over his laptop, he looked up at me and smiled. I smiled back. This most ancient of men was flirting with me. So I sat down on the sofa next to his chair and listened while he tried to explain Faro to me. He fairly giggled with excitement as he talked. And at one point, he winked at me, blushed, and said, "You look a lot like her, you know."

"Like who?"

"Oh, her – I forgot her name. She was. She was, oh who was she anyway? You look a lot like her." And with that, his head nodded and he fell asleep. I moved his laptop onto the end table and wondered that a man his age could be both ancient and modern.

"He was looking forward to seeing you again."

I turned, startled. I hadn't heard Chief Sorensen come in.

"Oh, Chief Sorensen. Or Randy." His sudden appearance left me unsure of what to say next.

"That depends." He smiled. He might have been more handsome if he hadn't looked so tired, and sad. Even smiling, his eyes told a different story. "Are we talking about murder or family history?"

"We could start with murder," I answered. I was surprised and pleased that he might actually talk to me about the murder. But after all, I had been the one who found the dead body, and it had happened at the home of my ancestors. I needed to know.

"Then you can call me Chief Sorensen for now." He dropped into a chair opposite me, yawned and rubbed his eyes.

"It might not even be a murder," he said. "The coroner is thinking natural causes, and the major case detectives are ending their investigation for now anyway."

"But you think it is murder?"

"Yes. I felt it the minute I arrived on the scene. There was nothing natural about it. I see too many unanswered questions. I'm continuing on my own. It's how I work best."

I hoped he didn't mean that –the working alone part. "Maybe you could use at least a teensy bit of help? " I held up a thumb and forefinger with only a hair of space between them. "I was married to a former prosecutor. I know a lot about evidence in murder cases. And I pay attention, and sometimes I notice things others miss. And, and, well maybe you'd let me tag along?" I blurted it all out. I don't know why. It was more than curiosity. I felt the way I used to feel as a newspaper reporter when I got my teeth into a good story. I was ready to go.

He looked at me and said nothing for what seemed like a very long time, then rubbed his eyes again and studied his knees. I waited.

He sighed and ran a hand again across his balding head. "OK, but only if you stay out of trouble and do what I tell you to do.

"Yes. Yes," I nodded my head up and down a bit too vigorously. "And maybe Audrey could help, too. She solves all the murders in the murder mysteries she reads."

"No. One tagalong is quite enough," he said, rising from his chair. "Either you or Audrey." He smiled, knowing my answer.

"Me then. What do we do first? Maybe we should drive out to the house where she was murdered….if she was murdered. We could do that now."

"I thought you were here to learn more about your ancestors."

"Well yes, but they've been dead for a long time, and as far as I know they weren't murdered." I felt a little disloyal to the cause that had brought me here. "Maybe we could just talk about what you know on the way."

This time he laughed. "I can tell you something you might find interested. You're not the only ancestor interested in Johannes and Karen. After I talked to you last, I started thinking about your story and thought it seemed familiar. I looked through my files and found letters or emails from six others asking for information about your great great grandparents. All of them had similar stories to yours, but each involved a slightly different interpretation. They'd all heard stories from their own parents or grandparents about money that belonged to either Johannes or Karen. They all thought one of them had hidden away a fortune somewhere or given it away. One thought Karen was a member of the Danish Royal Family. And another thought Johannes had a shady past going back to a gang of robbers in Denmark or maybe in America. Also something about a missing diary."

"And?"

"I told them as much as I've told you, and most seemed to lose interest. That happens a lot. People get busy or find something else to interest them. Or they learn all they need to know and don't want to learn more.

He stopped as if another idea had just crept into his consciousness. "Of course, they could all still be out there and still trying to learn more – just without me."

He shrugged his shoulders. "You've been the most persistent. You and one other."

That caught my attention. "Who is the other?" I had a couple suspicions of my own, but he surprised me with his answer."

"The woman in the morgue. Our murder victim."

My first thought was that she and I were both victims of a family curse. I wondered if she, like me, was running away as well as running to. Like me, maybe she thought the distant past more comfortable than the present or future. I said the obvious. "So she's a distant cousin. We have the same great great grandparents."

"Maybe, "Chief Sorensen answered, pointing towards the door. "We'll leave in a minute after I get my granddad down for a nap."

As he turned towards his grandfather, I asked him about his grandfather's last remark to me. "He said I looked just like someone. What did he mean by that?

He stopped what he was doing and looked out the window. "I don't know what he's talking about half the time." He hoisted his grandfather out of his chair and carried him in his arms like a baby.

Chapter 14

We had at least three hours before sunset, time enough to reach the house and look around – for what, I wasn't sure. I phoned Audrey to explain where I was. As I expected, she seemed both intrigued and unhappy. She was unhappy that I wouldn't be there to help with the evening feeding but curious about anything that I might learn – and jealous too, I'm sure. Not that she would ever say so. To Audrey, jealousy was an unnecessary emotion. But she did ask me to meet her later at Bella's.

I ended my call as Chief Sorensen backed out of his driveway with me in the passenger seat.

"So, have you identified the victim?"

"We found a driver's license with the name Lydia Harrison, so that's what I'm going with now."

That much I already knew.

"We found no identification for a Goldie La Chien or any other person."

That much I could have guessed.

"Lydia Harrison told the broker she was interested in buying the house but signed a rental agreement instead. She told the realtor that it was because she wanted to make sure she liked it here. From Bella's description of the woman who stayed at their place for a few days, we know that the woman who stayed at Bella's and the women in the morgue are the same person. We don't yet know anything about the woman who called herself Goldie La Chien. We don't even know if she's alive."

The plot thickens, I thought.

"I'll have fingerprint information tomorrow. That should confirm our identification of Lydia Harrison and might tell us something about her last visitors."

I thought about that for a while as we turned onto the country road that would lead us to our destination.

"And what will you be looking for here?" I asked as he pulled up to the yellow farm house I'd wanted to buy. I stepped out of the car onto a gravel path that echoed under my steps. As I looked towards the house, I once again had the sensation that the sky was slipping down around my shoulders. A hundred degrees at least today, and I shivered. Did I really want to be here?

Chief Sorensen touched my shoulder. "Are you ok?"

"I'm ok."

"You asked what I will be looking for. I'm not always sure, but sometimes the place itself speaks to me. I can pick up plenty of science from the crime scene techs, but I can learn even more by quietly looking around. Sometimes I even sit for a while with my eyes closed. So far I'm dealing with a couple ghosts that shared a bottle of wine."

If I were someone who could lift one eyebrow at a time, I would have done so then. This was a police chief, a detective, talking like a...like I don't know what, but not what I expected.

He saw the surprise in my eyes, the tilt of my head, and he laughed softly.

"I've taken a lot of ribbing over the years over my investigative strategies, but I've also solved a lot of murders."

"I'm ok with your style, or rather your investigative strategies."

"You haven't asked about my correspondence with Lydia Harrison. I thought that might interest you."

"Well, yes." I actually stopped just outside the front door and turned to face him." Do tell. What did she ask? Even more important, what did she know?"

As we stepped into the entry, he told me about the several emails he'd received a couple years ago. He'd answered five or six as best he could, and then the emails had ceased. Then a few weeks ago this same Lydia Harrison had called to talk to him personally and also to ask about buying or renting the farm house where her ancestors and mine had lived.

"She decided to rent initially. I never met her. The realtor mailed her the keys. So I can't even be sure if the dead woman is Lydia Harrison.

I was curious and asked about his correspondence with this distant and evidently now deceased relative.

"She mentioned much of what you told me, all the same family mysteries. She also wrote about her own great grandmother's diary, full of girlish crushes and daily activities but also with a few odd comments about hidden treasures and well-kept secrets. She repeated a phrase about curtains hiding the truth and walls holding their silence. Very poetic, I thought. But Lydia seemed to take them literally."

We'd walked past the table where I'd seen the wine glasses and empty bottle and into the kitchen. Chief Sorensen nodded at the large hole in the far wall. "See."

A hole with ragged edges and curls of dangling paint stretched a third of the way across the wall. The Chief poked his head cautiously inside and looked around. "Don't think she found anything here, but she did try. I wonder if she was planning to poke holes all over the house."

"Wouldn't make the landlord too happy," I said, adding, "And who does own this place?

He gave me one of those "you caught me" smiles and let me know that he, in fact, owned this place. I wanted to know how long he'd owned it and more, but he held up his hand and asked for silence.

"I need quiet. I need to look around and see what I might learn. I need to listen to what the house tells me.

OK. That sounded a little odd, but I let him get on with it while I spent some time looking around on my own. Outside of the house, I'd felt threatened. Inside, I felt comfortable in spite of the fact that a distant but unknown cousin of mine may have been murdered here. Nothing at all suggested to me what had happened. I sat for a while and passed my fingers over the sun yellow table cloth, thinking that a short time ago two people had shared wine and conversation here. Had they been friends? Enemies? Had Lydia been afraid and tried to calm her murderer with wine and conversation? Two people sitting at a table drinking wine. Why were they sitting around a table and not relaxing in the living room? Did they need the table? Were papers and books spread out before them, items that disappeared with the murderer? I could almost feel their presence, hear their voices.

I climbed the steep stairs hidden behind a door and found myself in a bedroom with a large 4-poster bed, an elegant bedspread with violets and lace, a tiny lamp on the bedside table, and almost nothing else. No pictures on the wall. No mess. Nothing piled haphazard on the dresser top. No scattered shoes or discarded items. The closet revealed only a few shirts, pants and dresses with plenty of space around them. Every item seemed new and expensive. In the dresser drawers, I found newly purchased and still unworn underwear. I've heard of people reinventing themselves and maybe that's what I was doing, but where had she come from, what had she done, who had she been?

And then, oddly, I longed for the confusion and the mess of life with Audrey and the rescue dogs. The quiet here tired me. When I was with Audrey, we both laughed and longed for the day when we could live in a home with intact furniture, everything clean, tidy, and welcoming. This place was clean and tidy but not welcoming.

I poked around the other rooms and closets upstairs, all unoccupied, unfurnished and empty. I stepped out on a balcony and looked out towards the lake in the distance. For a moment, I thought I saw a shadow move from behind a tree, but then it was gone. Finally I returned to the staircase and eased myself back downstairs, carefully navigating the narrow steps by hugging one wall with my hip and feeling for each new step in the dim light.

I found Chief Sorensen still sitting in the living room, elbows on his knees, head in his hands, eyes closed. I was afraid to interrupt him, so I sat down in a chair opposite and just stared at him for a while. This was one odd detective, I thought. Finally he lifted up his head and asked me why I thought she was murdered.

Me? I wasn't even sure she was murdered. The coroner thought it likely natural causes. But if she had been murdered, it probably had something to do with who she was before she came to Nebraska. Or maybe someone else thought there might be a fortune hidden here, and that person had killed her. That would make me a suspect, wouldn't it? I also was here trying to unravel the mysteries of Karen and Johannes. Why would I want anyone to beat me to the answers or to the hidden fortune which I suspected was all myth? I thought too that maybe she'd just died from loneliness, stretched out in the doorway, one arm reaching for the happiness that eluded her.

I I shared my thoughts with Chief Sorensen, and he nodded and hoisted himself out of the sofa.

"You haven't asked why I think this might be a murder and not natural causes?"

I didn't need to ask. He quickly explained his theory. The body in the doorway seemed posed. She was on her stomach, face to one side, one arm stretched out as if pointing into the distance or pointing at someone. People who die naturally have a different look about them, he said. Lack of blood and bruises made it all less obvious, but he felt sure he'd find something. As he spoke, he paced around the room.

Was there anything in the wine? Anything in her blood? He said he would know more about that soon – maybe today.

"So did the house tell you anything?"

"Maybe a little. I'll be back again. And tomorrow I should have finger print results and learn if her computer has anything to tell us."

So he wasn't going to share anything more with me today. And I was really beginning to wonder about his detecting skills. Had he really been a big city homicide cop? He stood gazing out a window. I followed his gaze and saw a man walking about the property waving a long-poled object back and forth on the ground in front of him.

"Isn't that Carl?" I asked, leaning forward and squinting.

"Yup. Carl and his metal detector. You should ask him about that. He's always out with that thing. He's especially fond of old farm houses where people used to bury their valuables....and then forget about them, I guess.

"Has he ever found anything?

"Ask him."

Chapter 15

The Killer

    I see them all floundering about, not understanding. That burn-out of a police chief. You can still smell the alcohol even if he has quit drinking. Not that I ever got that close. I'm careful. And now that odd woman from Missouri who only seems to own a couple changes of clothes. I see her flopping about just to make the time pass. One of these days she will fall over and stay down.

    And the dogs, the dogs, all those dogs. What is so important about rescuing dogs when so many people are drowning? Too many Dog Ladies, if you ask me. Too many Dog Gentlemen too. Driving here from Kansas, I thought about my next step. Then it all fell in place so easily.

    I'm taking a chance not leaving Redbud right away, but I'll be gone today before anyone notices me. . So far they're not seeing things clearly. They're not making the connection. I may need to enlighten them.

    Audrey thinks she's so smart and so clever. People think she's a character, think she's so wonderful. I know her better than any of them. She had her chance to help me, but now it's too late.

Chapter 16

I'd never seen Bella's so busy. Laughter spilled out the front door as a couple at the door poked their heads in for a quick look.

"Might be a long wait," the man said to his companion.

I slipped around them and squeezed through the door sideways, spotting Bella as she faced a tight crowd in one corner, all of them sipping from wine glasses and chattering loudly. "Enjoy your drinks," she beamed. "I'll have a table soon." She punctuated her words with hands in the air, as if she were adding a comma here, an exclamation point at the end. Then she raced back to the kitchen. I tried to catch her eye but failed. Bella's was no longer the cozy living room I'd first visited. Where did all these people come from? The answer came when I heard someone talking about the review he'd read online and how he'd driven an hour just to check it out.

Carl might have been in the kitchen. I couldn't spot him although I wanted to know about his metal detector and why he'd brought it to the murder site. In the corner I spotted Audrey and several of her volunteers. Audrey stood and waved one arm back and forth above her head. I zigzagged through the room, trying not to upend any of the tables, more than I'd ever seen crowded together in one room. On the sofa I saw four people eating from dishes balanced on their knees while talking to two others who stood nearby spearing bites from the plates they held.

"Isn't this wild? " Audrey asked as I finally found a seat at her table. "God, I hope they all hate their meals and say bad things about Bella's. I want my cozy diner back."

"But...," I started, and she waved a hand to stop me. "I don't mean it, of course. Carl and Bella deserve the recognition." She tilted her head as if rethinking her statement. "Actually, maybe I do hope these people never come back."

Audrey was again wearing some sort of flowing, flowery dress that looked like a sheet she might have just wrapped around herself and fastened with a belt. I had to admit it wasn't that bad. Eccentric, but not a bad look for her. Her earrings dangled past her shoulders. I was, as usual, in shorts and t-shirt. As I looked around, I realized I was way underdressed. Now I wanted all these people to go away and give me back the place where it didn't matter how I dressed.

Audrey interrupted my thoughts and spread her arms to include the two women with her. "We have a saying around here. 'All roads lead to Redbud.'" Audrey had my attention. "It's hard to find someone who doesn't at least know someone who's been to Redbud. Try it sometime – next time you're somewhere else. Six degrees of Redbud, I call it. You can be in Paris, talking to a complete stranger. That person will know someone who knows someone, who knows someone, who knows someone who's been to Redbud. Was that six? I lost count. Anyway, pretty good when you consider Redbud has a population of about 5,000 and is in a state no one wants to visit."

I laughed. Obviously, Audrey was not on her first glass of wine. Maybe she was even breaking her two glass rule. She glanced at me with questions to ask and whispered "later." Then she draped an arm around the woman next to her and introduced me to Lois James and Barbara Hansen. "These two are my best foster parents. My best. But they drive me nuts when they call their foster dogs "babies" and dress them up like dolls. They also wear jewelry and clothes decorated with dogs. Worse yet, they talk about the 'Rainbow Bridge' where dogs that have passed on wait to meet the humans who loved them. Oh please. Such excessive sentimentality."

Lois and Barbara just smiled and nodded. Lois was a tall, lean woman with short hair and glasses. Barbara, short and constantly smiling, said, "We admit it. And it's how we want to be. It's Audrey who's different."

Indeed. I already knew that Audrey was unlike most others in the rescue world. She was probably the least sentimental person I'd ever met. She rescued dogs. She cared for them well. She paid the bills. She found them homes. But I never saw her cry or refer to herself as a dog's "mummy." She literally scowled at a woman who once called her a "saint" for the good work she was doing for all the "poor puppies."

I couldn't tell if Audrey was really disapproving of Lois and Barbara or just having fun with them. She next told me that the two women also oohed and aahed and make all sorts of strange noises whenever they saw other people's babies.

Lois and Barbara both nodded. "Guilty again," said Barbara, "and don't let Audrey tell you she doesn't like babies. She had one of her own once."

"That's different. Of course I loved my own child and still do now that she's no longer a child. But I'll tell you a secret. I loved her a little more every year....not just when she was a baby."

I was hungry and trying to catch the attention of the teenaged waitress darting from table to table. I was confused. "What," I asked, "does ogling babies have to do with dogs and dog rescue?" I asked.

"Everything," said Audrey, smacking her hand on the table. "Sentimentality gets in the way, whether you're raising children or rescuing dogs. Sentimentality is dishonest. Life requires honesty and good hard work and authentic feeling. We don't need all that sugary mush."

Dear God, I thought, do I really need more honesty in my life or more authentic feeling. I refused to cry. I couldn't stand another word about babies. Didn't they know about mine? And then I realized, they didn't. As far as I knew, they knew nothing about my personal tragedies. I felt a little better, relieved that I wouldn't see in their eyes the look I'd grown to dread.

"Let's order," I said, and as if my magic, the young waitress appeared at our table.

An hour later, we were satisfied and still running forks around the edges of our plates, scooping up just a little more flavor. "Bella and Carl really outdid themselves," I said.

Lois yawned and got to her feet with Barbara rising soon after. "We need to go. Nice to meet you, Judy, and don't let Audrey scare you away from dog clothes and dog earrings. Sometimes these things are just fun." During our dinner I'd learned that both Lois and Barbara were school teachers with children who were now away at college. By fostering rescue dogs, they were still mothering something. Both women kissed Audrey on the cheek, although she grimaced when they did so. Both patted me on the back. "Get some sleep, both of you," Lois whispered my way.

As the two women walked out of Bella's, Audrey turned to me. "So talk. What do you know?"

I told her about my trip with Chief Sorensen and what I'd seen in the house.

"So he really thinks she was murdered. Did he say why?"

"That was strange. It was like he could just tell by looking that death was not from natural causes. He thought the corpse had been posed with one arm reaching out as if pointing somewhere.

"What direction?"

"What direction what?"

"What direction was she pointing?"

I thought about it. The arms was pointing in the direction of the road to Audrey's.

I told her, and she just nodded.

"Chief Sorensen. He's kind of an odd man – nice, but a little odd," I added

Audrey agreed. "He is a little strange, but he's a good detective. He does know what he's doing. Give him some time. You'll see. "

Then I noticed Carl coming into the restaurant. Odd that he'd been gone during such a busy evening. He seemed in a hurry to find Bella.

I almost bumped heads with Audrey as I bent towards her and whispered. "Carl was out there. We saw him near the lake with a metal detector."

Before she could answer, both Carl and Bella pulled out the vacant chairs at our table and joined us.

After Audrey complimented them on the successful evening, she grew silent. I told Carl I'd seen him earlier out with his metal detector. He raised an eyebrow and slid a glance Bella's way. I looked from one to the other, waiting for a response. Instead, everyone suddenly seemed uncomfortable.

"Oh, it's nothing," Bella finally said, waving an arm grandly towards Carl. "It's just Carl's silly hobby. He keep finding little trinkets and arrowheads, and you'd be surprised how many coins fall out of pockets."

Then Audrey stood up and tapped me on the shoulder. "Time to go. We have some anxious dogs waiting for their bedtime romp in the yard."

Bella and Carl stared after us as we left.

Chapter 17

That night I dreamed I was back in college, but I'd lost my class schedule. I plowed through the papers in my purse. Not there. Someone offered me another purse, also stuffed full of receipts, folded notes, cards, envelopes. Not there either. I asked my mother for help, but realized she really wasn't my mother. I'd also lost a ticket to a movie about puppy mills. Finally, I asked directions to an office where someone might help me with my schedule. I was waiting in line there when I woke up.

Waking up at Audrey's is always the same. Only the dogs on my bed change. This morning an Australian Shepherd scratched at my head. A chocolate lab snored at my feet, and a black and white beagle mix curled near the small of my back. A scruffy black dog stood on his back legs next to my bed, his paws near my face. When the first thing you see in the morning is a monkey-faced dog, well it can be a little alarming.

As usual, I heard Audrey clattering away in the kitchen and whistling softly, I knew I should get up.

We tackled our morning chores pretty much in silence except for our clucks, hellos, comes, good boys, good girls, no no's, downs, offs, whistles and more as we fed our crew and supervised their morning playtime. The telephone rang and Audrey answered several calls without much conversation. After a quick mopping and dusting, I began scrolling through emails and answering or forwarding to other foster homes the usual inquiries about our adoptable dogs. As for the request that we take certain dogs from shelters or owners, I printed them out and tucked them in a file for Audrey.

Up until today I'd always seen Audrey as peaceful if not exactly joyful. She was, to use her own word, "authentic." She lived without complaint or pessimism, without drama or outrage. She showed her displeasure with some light huffing, but she did not dwell much on the evils of humanity. Instead she believed that the world was a little bit better today than yesterday. She saw progress where others saw defeat. When others complained about cruelty to animals, she nodded but then pointed out the big picture, the statistics that showed fewer substandard puppy mills and fewer homeless dogs. Most states recorded dramatic drops in the number of dogs being euthanized in shelters, she was quick to point out. She celebrated and shared the figures and embraced her own part in the progress. Every day I lived with Audrey, I felt slightly more anchored.

Except for today. Today I felt fluttery, airborne. Audrey was not the Audrey who'd pulled me into her home and her life. She was more than just silent. She was distant, diminished. I tried to say something, but the look in her eyes silenced me. So I waited. I waited for Audrey, and I waited to hear from Chief Sorensen.

Finally, Audrey pulled a chair next to me as I was trying to write a blog about Madge, an elderly Golden mix who would stare at her dog bed and bark without stopping until someone cleared a toy or piece of paper off her spot. Then she'd quiet herself, step onto the bed, massage it a bit, and collapse with a sigh, closing her eyes instantly.

"There's something I should tell you now. You'll find out soon enough."

I turned to look at her, afraid of what I might hear.

"I'm pretty sure the woman who called herself Goldie La Chien was my sister or maybe I should say my long lost sister. I haven't seen her in more than 20 years. I tried to reach out to her when she had all the problems with her son. That's another story. She had, shall we say, a complicated life, and she blamed me for some of her problems. We had a big blowup long ago and I was relieved to have her out of sight and mind. Later I wished I'd kept in touch more. Then came the trouble. When I tried to help her, she rejected any offers. Then a year ago she called out of the blue. I told her what I was doing. She couldn't believe anyone would want to live with even one dog."

"Not a dog person, huh? I can remember a time not long ago when I might have felt the same way."

"Well, she called a few more times and joked that she might just be a Dog Lady herself one day. She said she might change her name to Goldie La Chien."

"Oh! So that's how you knew. She used that name so you'd know she was here."

"And I should have rushed right out to welcome her, to let her know that I cared, to try to fix things between us. But I needed time to think about how to approach her, what to say, and so I put it off. Now it's too late."

I opened my mouth but couldn't think of a response. Then I remembered something. "But we didn't really know where this Goldie La Chien was staying."

"I could have found her. At the farmhouse or the motel maybe." She looked at the ceiling. I expected a tear to roll down one cheek. Audrey misted up but seldom cried. One tiny tear broke loose, and she wiped it away.

"She was my sister. We had our problems but I tried to help her through the bad times."

The bad times? Again, something about bad times. I thought she would tell me more, but my cellphone rang. Audrey took the interruption as an opportunity to slip away to spend more time with some of the dogs downstairs. "Later," she said. I was beginning to think that was her favorite word. Later.

I swiped my cellphone and answered. It was Chief Sorensen.

"Turn on the television."

I turned on the television and saw the words scrolling across the bottom of the screen. "Breaking News: Killer claims responsibility for two poisoning deaths. Warns there will be more. Stay tuned."

The screen blackened and came back on with an announcer looking out from behind a news desk.

"Television stations in Topeka and Omaha today received messages from an anonymous writer claiming responsibility for two recent deaths. The message said both women died of phenobarbital poisoning. The message warned of future deaths and named the two victims as Michelle Ames from the Topeka area and Lydia Harrison, who had recently moved to Redbud, Nebraska, from New York City. Ms. Ames operated a dog rescue organization outside of Topeka and Lydia Harrison

61

recently retired as chief operating officer of a dog shelter outside of New York City."

The announcer paused and frowned. "Where a signature might have been, the message closed with the words "Death to the Dog Ladies."

"Your Midlands News Team will have more on this breaking story at 6."

Oh my God. Oh my God. Death to the Dog Ladies? Death to the Dog Ladies! Audrey had stepped up next to me as soon as the announcer began speaking. I looked at her. She pressed her lips together tightly and narrowed her eyes.

My phone rang again. Chief Sorensen suggested meeting him at the murder site. He'll tell us all he knows so far. Audrey decided to stay home but waved me out the door.

Chapter 18

I was halfway to the murder site when I slammed on the brakes and skidded to the side of the road. How could I be so slow to see the truth! I bumped my head against the steering wheel a few times to wake my brain.

Chief Sorensen had told me Lydia Harrison had emailed him about my ancestors Johannes and Karen. If they were also her ancestors, she and I were distant relatives. And what about Audrey? Was she another distant cousin?

I did a little mental math. Johannes and Karen had eleven children, eight of whom lived long enough to have children of their own. These eight averaged about 7 children each. And although each generation produced fewer children per person, the total was several hundred by now....several hundred or maybe more than a thousand all claiming Johannes and Karen as ancestors. The numbers rattled around in my head. How many people might be thinking about the same stories I'd heard growing up. How many were searching ancestry.com and consulting genealogists. How many had visited Redbud? How many lived here? I knew only a couple cousins from my mother's side of the family and I didn't know them well.

Hundreds. Hundreds. Maybe a thousand. Whatever made me think I was unique, the only one curious about a bunch of family stories? I pulled back onto the highway and continued thinking.

And what if curiosity killed Lydia Harrison? Curiosity about her ancestors and the stories of lost wealth and hidden treasures. I tossed that idea about a bit. I was almost to the farm when another thought sliced through me like lightening.

Chief Sorensen! Chief Sorensen owned the property. Why? An innocent investment? An inheritance? A deliberate purchase so he could chase down his own family stories which might just also be my stories? And how well had he known Lydia Harrison?

I screeched to a stop at the yellow farm house and bounded out of the car, not bothering to slam the door shut. I caught up with Chief

Sorensen in the back yard where he seemed to be gazing lazily out at the lake. I punched his shoulder, and he yelped and jumped back from me.

"What the..."

"What is this game you're playing?!"

"Game?" He looked a little mystified.

"Are you also one of my distant cousins? Is this whole town just one incestuous pool of people who trace back to the same ancestors? And are you all just laughing at me and my ignorance?" I actually stomped my foot, a childish action, I know, but I needed something more than a raised voice. And besides my voice was starting to quiver, and Chief Sorensen was fighting back a smile.

"Did you just now discover the link between you and Audrey?" He actually chuckled. I'd never known anyone who could made a sound that was unmistakably a chuckle.

And actually I hadn't made the connection – not definitely anyway -- until just this moment. "So Audrey is a distant cousin too? And her sister?"

He kicked at some stones in the yard. Sort of an "oh shucks I'm just a country boy" act. "And here I thought Audrey had invited you here. She told me she was helping you get over some tough times and you were helping her with the dogs."

Tough times. Bad times. Maybe she thought she'd do for me what she hadn't done for her sister. But stop. Wait. "That's not exactly how it happened." And I told him of my first encounter with Audrey, how I'd shown up at her door with a check I'd found made out to Redbud Area Dog Rescue. She'd practically pulled me into the house.

"Was that before or after you told her you were researching your ancestors?"

I thought for a moment. I wasn't really sure, but I remembered answering a question about what had brought me to Redbud. So maybe I did, and maybe I even mentioned the names of my ancestors. And maybe that all happened just before she reached for my hand. I was pretty sure I'd never said anything about the losses in my life, my other reason for leaving St. Louis. And yet Audrey seemed to know everything. I didn't need to answer Chief's Sorensen's question.

64

He nodded his head towards the back door and I followed him inside. As we stood awhile in the kitchen, he told me Audrey was a compassionate person (which I knew) who would hate to have anyone say she was compassionate (I knew that too). But Audrey had her own secrets. "But I don't understand why she wasn't straight with you."

He dropped into a chair next to the kitchen table and folded his hands almost prayer-like. "I have learned a few things."

I slipped into the chair next to him.

"As you know by now, we're no longer talking about natural causes here or in Topeka. We're talking about murder. We suspect that in each case the victim drank a glass of wine that had been laced with a lethal dose of phenobarbital."

I knew about phenobarbital because I was giving the drug to a dog named Olaf who had a seizure disorder. I also remembered that a famous model had committed suicide with phenobarbital and that members of a religious cult in California had committed mass suicide by drinking juice containing lethal doses of the barbiturate.

Chief Sorensen reminded me that phenobarbital was usually prescribed to treat insomnia, anxiety or seizure disorders.

The Chief said he'd never really considered suicide in this case. Lydia Harrison had recently moved here. She was starting a new life. Why now? Besides, the body seemed posed, the way it stretched out of the house with one arm pointing towards the road.

"I need to talk to Audrey again," he said, "I was hoping she'd come with you. I know her sister had called her recently. Audrey admitted as much but said they just talked about family stuff, nothing important."

That got me thinking that all the really important stuff, the good stuff and the bad stuff too was usually just family stuff. That's where you find the pain and the passion, the joy and the despair. And the loss. Always the loss.

"There's more," the Chief paused. "We found three sets of finger prints. The victim really is Lydia Harrison, and that really is her name. She really was head of a dog shelter outside of New York City." He sighed."

My mouth dropped open. "She really was a Dog Lady – although maybe not the kind that cleaned up dog poo. But what about the other prints? What did you learn about then? Was one of them Audrey's sister – the one who called herself Goldie La Chien?"

He shrugged his shoulders and told me what he knew about the other prints. One set belonged to a man named Charles Nesbitt. The others matched a woman who might be Audrey's sister. If that is Audrey's sister, she was presumed dead in 2001. "I'm hoping Audrey can enlighten me."

We're trying to locate this Charles Nesbitt. He may not be important. He might even be someone who helped pack the wine glasses. Or Lydia could have had other visitors

"And the person presumed dead?"

"She was in one of the Twin Towers on 9/11. She was never found. She never returned home. The company she'd worked for – a brokerage firm – had finger printed all its employees. That's how we had the ID. We think she is Audrey's sister. And we don't know where she is or if she might be yet another victim."

I knew that the only car left behind was one rented to Lydia Harrison.

But why, I wondered, would someone survive the terrorist assault of September 11, 2001, and just disappear? And how does someone stay disappeared?

As if to answer my question, the Chief said that the woman we thought was Audrey's sister never used any of her credit cards again, never applied for a job, and never opened a checking account in her name. She lived, as some say, "off the grid."

So where do we go from here? I wondered.

The Chief said he'd be talking to Audrey again, and I thought it was about time I talked to Audrey again too. Something wasn't right.

"And let's remember that Lydia claimed Karen and Johannes as her ancestors. So do Audrey and her sister….and you and a lot of other distant cousins."

Something about the sister's story fascinated me. I understood the whole idea of walking away, disappearing into the world, becoming someone else. For wasn't that what I was doing now? Except that I hadn't really disappeared. Anyone who wanted to find me still could. I had the same name, the same email, the same social security number.

"So why are we here?" I looked out the window towards the lake.

The Chief said he thought I might want to look around some more, get some ideas about my ancestors' home. He also hoped I might know more about Audrey's sister.

I told him what I did know and about the "bad times" that Audrey mentioned without telling me more. So far I didn't even know the sister's real name.

"I can find that out," the Chief said. "But for now, let's look around a little."

We looked first in the basement where we found a boarded up room. After pulling back some lose boards, the Chief opened enough space for us to step inside.   If we were expecting jewels, we didn't find them. Instead we found several pieces of rugged furniture and a few wood carvings, plus old tools that a carpenter might have used. One chair in particular looked familiar. I had one much like it in storage in St. Louis. I'd inherited it from my grandmother. It wasn't such a great chair, but I'd always liked the carvings that made it so unusual. It must have belonged to my ancestors; perhaps Johannes Jensen made it.

The Chief tipped the chair back a bit. "Heavy," he murmured. "Really solid." We looked at some of the other furniture, all of it with similar carvings. "Someone cared about his work."

I missed my similar chair and decided to drive back to St. Louis soon to get it out of storage.

Then I remembered the question the Chief hadn't answered.

"So are you another of my distant cousins?"

He laughed. "Not that I know. I inherited this place from my granddad who said his dad bought it and he wasn't sure who from. He's a crafty old guy, my granddad, so maybe he knows more than he's telling."

"He does say I remind him of someone."

'Hmmm. That is odd."

By now we were back outside and walking towards the lake. I saw in the distance a few dilapidated buildings, what might have been storage sheds or even barns at one time. I asked about them.

"Should have been torn down long ago. Nothing in them. I looked."

I insisted, and we hiked over to them. Inside we found nothing but an old chair, an ugly one at that, maybe an early effort when Johannes or someone else was learning to make furniture. We walked back towards the lake and watched two ducks rapidly tip-toeing along the surface as they reached for air and altitude, then disappeared into the sky, circling once before leaving the lake barren and still. Was this a sign summer heat might soon be leaving too?

"Oh," before you go, I found something." The chief pulled a folded paper out of one pocket and opened it to reveal a copy of an old newspaper article. I took the paper from him and started reading a piece about frontier gamblers in Nebraska.

"It might not be anything," he said as I read down the page, spotting names of some of the famous frontier gamblers and lawmen. Near the bottom I found a paragraph that began "And the biggest winner of them all was a mystery man known as Jos the Dane, so named because he always signed his name 'Jos' and didn't hide his immigrant status. Maybe he was just a card playing genius or maybe he was just lucky, but on those rare days that Jos the Dane asked to sit in, others groaned and some left." The article went on to report that no one knew where Jos the Dane called home. He'd show up one day and usually leave the next. Then he'd reappear months later for another short stay and almost always another big win. He wasn't just lucky with cards. "He always managed to leave town with all his winnings and his skin intact," the article concluded.

"But you do think it might be something, don't you?" I felt a shiver trailing up my spine.

"I also found the deed for the farmland he purchased from Union Pacific Railroad."

He paused.

"He signed his name Jos."

Chapter 19

In my dream I saw an infant crawling down a sidewalk alone, lost. Where were its parents? I'm sitting on a bus bench, waiting. No one cones running from either direction. The baby looks at me, turns, pushes itself up and lands happily on his diaper. He claps his hands and giggles and blows more giggles in my direction. I see a thousand words "giggle" floating through the air. Then the scene changes. I am now strapping my own baby into his car seat, kissing his forehead softly so not to wake him. I trot back into the house, grab my purse and peck my husband on the cheek as he straightens his tie. "Stay cool today," I coo. "It's supposed to be a scorcher." I wake up shaking.

Faith the Maltese brushed against my cheek, and I lifted her onto my chest. "What do you think we should do, little one? Should we start our day early?" I didn't want to stay in bed any longer, didn't want to fall back into that dream. I carried Faith outdoors for a bathroom visit; the other dogs on my bed dragged themselves out with me. But I wasn't yet ready to officially start the day.

Audrey was still in bed. I decided to spend a little time on the computer before I began the whole feeding and exercising process. I wanted to learn more about how a person could just disappear….and why.

Turns out there are websites and books advising people who want to disappear. It isn't easy, but if you really need to leave your past behind, you can do it. First you need to get rid of your credit cards. You use a credit card, and someone can find you. You also can't open a checking account in your name, or apply for a job in your field. You have to leave behind all your old hobbies, never again to go on a bird watching trip or take a yoga classes – if those are things you did in the past. If you were a lawyer before, you can't even work in a law office. If you were a newspaper reporter, forget about that. You probably can't even be a mystery writer under a pen name. Someone will recognize your style or a detail or two in your books. And if you were a stockbroker, you should stay away from any careers that involve investing money, even if you're just cleaning the offices. Someone will find you if you stick to what you've done in the past. You can't dress the same way, especially if you have an addiction to certain shoes or favorite designers. Someone will find you.

And then there's the internet. You simply can't be there. No Facebook page. No Blog. Lose your old email. No phone number that will trace back to you. The only cellphone you can own is one of those throwaway phones. You can't call your old friends or family. You can't subscribe to your favorite magazines or newspapers. You pay for everything with cash. If you run out of money, you must find jobs that pay in cash.

You can change your name and even get a new social security number, but the books and websites advise against stealing someone else's identity. Too tricky, unless you're the government setting someone up in a witness protection program, I guess. You can set up a corporation with your real name hidden way down in the incorporation paperwork. With that you are harder to find but are still able to do business, manage money and pay bills all in the name of the corporation.

It all sounded both interesting and lonely. What you did when you disappeared also depended on how important it was that no one ever finds you. Are you running from the law? Running away from creditors? Are you running from someone who wants to kill you? Or are you just starting over away from your horrible family and your bad influence friends? Or are you trying to stay ahead of the sadness that's chasing you. Or does a new start just seem romantic?

Some people disappear knowing that someone could find them eventually with enough time, work, and the help of a professional investigator. They just don't think anyone cares enough to go to the trouble. Others disappear knowing that discovery could mean death or disaster either for them or for others.

So why did Audrey's sister (Goldie La Chien?) walk away from her former life? Why did she decide to live "off the grid"?

I shut down the computer as I heard Audrey moving about in her room. Will she answer my questions? Will she tell me the truth?

"Judy," she says. "Could you take care of all the morning chores yourself? I have some important errands to run." And without another word, she brushed past me in an ankle-length sundress and with a white baseball cap on her head. Bracelets glittered on one wrist and earrings swayed and sparkled. I'd barely opened my mouth to speak and she was already backing out of the driveway in the Redbud Area Dog Rescue van. I sighed and went to work. Within an hour, I'd fed all the dogs and was now out playing in the yard with several of the more active ones. Everyone had been outside for bathroom breaks, and a few had decided to go back to bed. I still wasn't a dog person, but throwing a ball for a dog wasn't the worst way to start the day. The little dogs were all outside in the smaller yard, sniffing after one another and barking at the fence line dividing the small dogs from the bigger ones. Fences make for brave little dogs.

Usually Audrey and I would each spend some time with the small dogs and the big ones. Then we'd begin a quick mopping and cleaning, throwing dog bedding into the washing machine, bathing a dirty dog or two. Audrey was never one to take on more dogs than she could handle, so we could manage the work easily together. Alone, I struggled. The phone started ringing about 9, and I took down messages including one from Bella who said she needed to see Audrey RIGHT AWAY. Barbara and Lois both called to report that their latest foster dogs were darling and would be ready for adoption in a couple weeks. Someone called to see if we could do something about two dogs that had been abandoned in a back yard when the neighbors moved out. Someone else wanted us to take her two Chihuahuas because she was losing her home. Another caller had taken in her brother's dogs but couldn't afford them and couldn't get rid of the fleas, either.

How could Audrey stand this? I wondered. She'd always been the one answering the phone.

I turned to the emails. More of the same. Someone sent several pictures of a Jack Russell Terrier that was not getting along with the one-year-old human. One of the volunteers was going on vacation and needed someone to take her foster dogs. Another was setting up an adoption event and needed details about which dogs would be there.

Several people wanted application forms for dogs they'd seen on our website.

Done with the emails I decided to forget about a blog. Later I'd write about Scarlet No'Hara, a plain black dog who'd come to us nearly hairless from neglect and a skin infection. I ran my fingers over the short bristles beginning to break through on her rump. Luxurious her coat was not, but give it time and it will match her rich and loving spirit. She was smart too, quickly learning all her doggy manners, including perfect housebreaking, sit, stay, and leash walking. To be honest, she still needed help with the leash walking, a venture she found excessively exciting. I'd been the one to take her out of one of our local shelters. In her condition, her likelihood of finding a home was nonexistent, so she was on the morning list for euthanasia. When I said Redbud Area Dog Rescue would take her, several staff members and volunteers hugged me. They'd all been hoping this sweet but ugly dog would somehow find an angel. That day I was an angel.

Audrey had sent me to the shelter to check out the dogs, not to bring one home. But she forgave me when she saw the dog and heard her story. Audrey dreamed up the name Scarlet No'Haira. Next step, the vet office, and I volunteered for that too. We came home with meds for bacterial and fungal infections and special shampoo for her baths.

Now I had two dogs that I thought of as my own personal rescues: Faith the Maltese from the puppy mill shutdown, and now Scarlet No'Hara.

"Ready for a walk, Scarlet?"

And so we walked, and when we arrived back home we both jumped into the pool. Scarlet's first reaction was shock, followed quickly by delight. She swam awkwardly at first, slapping the surface and snapping at the bubbles she created. Later she discovered her lab- given talent and paddled gracefully and happily, circling around me as I floated on my back, thinking about what I'd learned from Chief Sorensen, trying to create a picture out of all the puzzle pieces, worrying that Audrey might never return.

As my thoughts darkened, so did the sky. Suddenly the wind whirled about us, blowing away the heat, blasting us with warnings of cold days to come. We scrambled from the pool and raced for the house.

Back inside, I crawled into bed with several quaking dogs as lightning crashed and windows rattled. I pulled the spread over my head; Faith burrowed down to my knees. Scarlet sat upright and tense, growling a warning to the wind.

Chapter 20

Audrey did not come home that night, nor the next morning. She didn't answer her cellphone. I called Chief Sorensen and a few of the volunteers. I worked and I waited. I struggled through dog chores. I yelled at dogs. I screamed "quiet!" and practiced angry tirades for when Audrey would finally appear. "How could you!" I'd yell. "What were you thinking?! How could you just run off like that and not let me know when you'd be back!" I was working up a good steam to drive off my cold fear.

By late afternoon, she was still missing. Desperate to do something, I left for Bella's. I would sit on Bella and Carl if I had to. I'd learn something from them.

I found them huddled around a small oval table near the kitchen. Carl's eyes were on his hands which rested on the table. Bella seems almost to be spitting out words and batting them away as if they were flies. When they saw me stomping towards them, they both froze, and Bella covered her mouth. I dragged a chair behind me, turned it towards then and dropped into it.

"It's time someone told me what's going on," I said.

They looked at each other.

"You do know that Audrey's missing, don't you? And you do know that the woman you knew as Goldie La Chien is most likely Audrey's sister. And you probably know that Audrey and her sister are descendants of my ancestors, Johannes and Karen."

They both nodded.

"And you do know that Audrey hadn't seen her sister for more than 20 years and that her sister had pulled a disappearing act after 911. What's going on? What don't I know?" I could hear my voice growing louder and shriller. "And now I suppose you'll tell me that you're some of my distant cousins too."

"Only one of us." Carl smiled. "Only me."

It's a good thing I was already sitting.

"Ok." Now I could only whisper. "Tell me more."

Carl took a deep breath and launched into a story much like my own. He and Bella had suffered a catastrophic loss when their two children both died in a school bus accident. They struggled to pull themselves together but found themselves more and more isolated from the people who had been their friends and co-workers.

"It was like people thought our loss might be contagious, something they could catch," Bella said.

Carl put his hand on her arm. "Or maybe they just didn't know what to say."

So one day they decided to leave New York and start over someplace else where no one knew their story.

"So you decided to move from New York City to Redbud, Nebraska?" Even I didn't quite believe that.

Carl continued his story. They sold their condo and started driving across the country with no real plan. One day they crossed the Missouri River and Carl remembered that some of his ancestors had settled in Nebraska in the 1870s. His grandmother had told him stories about her parents or maybe it was her grandparents on a farm near Redbud, Nebraska. She'd told him that someday he should visit the farm and he might find some treasures there. She told him many times to visit the farm of Johannes and Karen Jensen. As Carl grew older, he figured his grandma just loved entertaining him with a good story.

"I never took her seriously, but suddenly here we were. Bella thought we might as well stop and look around a bit. Then a funny thing happened. We fell in love with this town and decided to stay." He threw out his arms wide. "And here we are, and here's Bella's."

"And then you met Audrey," I said, wanting to hear the rest of the story.

"And then we met Audrey." He agreed. "But not right away. We'd heard of her and her dog rescue group. Half the town seemed to be fostering dogs for her. But it wasn't until Bella's opening day that we actually met Audrey. Then Bella's became her favorite retreat, and we all became friends."

I asked when they found out Carl and Audrey were distant cousins, and Bella pitched in with the story of how Audrey had asked

76

them how in the world they could have ended up in Redbud. "When Carl told her about his grandma and her stories, Audrey laughed until tears rolled down her cheeks."

"Then she told us to just forget about thinking we'd find any hidden treasure on the old Jensen place. She could barely talk she was laughing so hard, but finally we understood that she too was descended from Karen and Johannes and that her grandma had also told her stories about hidden treasures. But *her* grandma talked about pearls Karen had received as a gift from the Queen of Denmark. Audrey had done her share of research, it seems, but had decided that all the stories were just that – stories. And even if Karen or Johannes had buried a few coins or pearls, someone else would have found them a couple generations ago. And face it, she'd said, these were poor immigrants. What they thought of as a fortune might be laughably paltry today."

I wondered if that really was Audrey's opinion. She hadn't told me the same thing. Even after I'd told her I was researching my ancestors, she'd kept quiet. Why had she revealed all to Carl and Bella but nothing to me?

"Carl didn't give up, though," said Bella. "You saw him out there with his metal detector."

"A guy's got to dream," Carl sighed. He nodded my way as if telling a secret. "And I don't for a minute believe Audrey isn't curious about what might be out there too. She's got her own collection of papers and stories, some of which she's shared with us."

But not with me, I thought.

I asked the question I should have asked first. "Do you have any idea where she is?"

Again, they both looked at each other before Carl spoke.

"We know she was upset.....and scared too, I think. She said she had something she needed to do. I think she was going to see someone."

"Do you think she's ok? And if she is, why hasn't she called? Why doesn't she answer her phone?"

"We think she's ok. We hope so." He hesitated. "But we haven't heard from her either."

As I stood up to leave, I thought for a moment Bella had something more to say. Both hands floated upwards as if in surrender. But just then Carl touched her arm and the hands dropped back onto the table.

Before I began my drive back, I called Chief Sorensen and told him Audrey was still not back home and I was worried. He didn't tell me I had nothing to worry about. I was hoping he would. Instead, he said he'd learned something new and was following a hunch about where Audrey might have gone. He'd let me know more when he knew more.

Chapter 21

As I pulled into the driveway, I saw golden light shining through every window in the house and several people scurrying around inside. The dogs in the yard yelped at the fence line as I opened the car door. Someone stepped out on the porch and called my name. She appeared as a shadow outlined by the light from within. Gradually, I recognized Barbara, one of the retired teachers now fostering dogs for Redbud Area Dog Rescue.

"We're here to help. Lois and I will be staying with you until Audrey returns. Lois is unpacking now. And a few of the other volunteers have been feeding the dogs and taking them outside."

As if summoned, a line of women and one man joined Barbara on the porch, lining up as if they were a church choir preparing to sing. Some even folded their hands in front of them. To a soul, they all appeared frightened.

"Thank you. Thank you." As much as I tried to appear calm and unafraid, I felt moisture on my cheeks. And then my two special rescue dogs – Faith the puppy mill Maltese and Scarlett the formerly hairless lab mix – pushed their heads between two of the choristers and bolted in my direction. I scooped up Faith and kneeled to hug the lab whose hair was now a mass of new growth with the consistency of sand paper. Hiding my head in the dogs, I hoped no one could see my tears and my fear.

Then I stood and I told them what I knew and that Chief Sorensen was following a hunch as to where Audrey might be. I'd talked with Carl and Bella and neither of them had any idea of where Audrey might be. "But they both thought she was ok," I offered, not fully believing my words.

"Goldie La Chien was Audrey's sister?" Barbara asked, her mouth hanging open. Others nodded, a sort of shared disbelief. How could this be?

The perfect choir line loosened as some stepped back inside and others huddled together in apparent deep discussion.

I turned to Barbara, who shook her head and said, "I thought I knew everything about her." She paused. "But I knew she had her secrets. She described herself as a 'very private person.' Maybe that was her way of not inviting too many questions."

I nodded, realizing Audrey had never really talked much about herself. It was always about the dogs. She also never asked me about my past, even though I showed up on her home in obvious need of rescue. She had reached out her hand, pulled me through the door and literally tucked me into a new life. Not such a bad thing.

An hour later, the others left and Lois, Barbara and I finished a few more chores. Finally, with the dogs put into their kennels and dog dishes soaking in the sink, the three of us settled down in the living room to talk. Lois wore a t-shirt that said "Dogs are People Too." Barbara had earrings shaped like schnauzers. These were the sentimental girls Audrey loved to tease. Now they seemed very no-nonsense, ready to get to work finding Audrey and returning Redbud to its proper place as a safe harbor for residents and visitors alike.

But where to begin? We needed to figure out where she might have gone? We wondered if the person who had killed Lydia Harrison had really meant to kill Audrey. And what did Audrey know she wasn't sharing? Was her sister another victim? Did Audrey know who might be responsible for the dog lady murders?

And where was Audrey? Why did she run?

Was she running from something or to something?

Both Barbara and Lois knew about Audrey's ancestors (and mine). They also knew there was some mystery about hidden wealth.

Barbara said, "My grandmother went to school with one of the younger Jensen girls. She had a few stories about Karen, the mother, and Johannes too. She said Johannes was well-liked, clever and hard-working but a little 'rough around the edges.' She wasn't sure he could even read or write."

"Is he the one they said always told stories about his travels through the Old West?" asked Lois.

"That's the one." Barbara explained that the Jensen's were among the original settlers, so people were always trying to learn more

80

about them and the other early immigrants. School children were always being sent out to interview the oldest people in the town to mine their memories and more. "I'm not sure how much truth came out of any of that."

I thought for a while about the family stories that sometimes turn out to be family myths leading us down paths to nowhere. And yet somehow I felt that the dog lady murders and Audrey's disappearance were connected somehow to the past, to the history of Johannes and Karen. But how I didn't know.

Barbara continued her story, "As for Karen, she was almost the opposite of Johannes. She was well-educated, dignified in manner and sometimes a little aloof, although some just thought she was shy and secretive."

But how does any of this history help us find Audrey or find the murderer in our midst?

Lois leaned back in her recliner and closed her eyes. I thought she might be falling asleep, but she was just organizing her thoughts.

"I don't think Audrey saw herself the way we all see her. I know I think of her as a confident, take charge, successful person. But when I complimented her one time on all she'd done, she stared at me like she'd just discovered I was a total idiot.

"What did she say?"

"Maybe the most revealing thing she ever did say to me or anybody else. She laughed at first and said she usually thought of herself as a loser, someone who could have done a lot better with her life. She was sure than when she died, her finally thoughts would not be of her successes but of her failures and her regrets."

Barbara and I remained silent, waiting for the rest of the story.

"That's it. Then she changed the subject and went back to work taking care of the dogs."

I smiled. It was like hearing Audrey's voice. Forget everything else. Just take care of the dogs.

But I couldn't forget everything else – not in my life or in hers. But I knew what I needed to do tomorrow. I would talk to the oldest person in town. And I knew where to find him.

81

Chapter 22

I dreamed I was in France and had lost my passport. I couldn't go anywhere without it, not even to a theatre. I applied for a new one, but when it arrived the picture on it was not of me. I tried to call someone about the problem but couldn't remember how to use my phone. I asked people around me for help, but no one else could figure out how to make a call either. I climbed on a bus that I thought would take me to the office where I could show someone the wrong face on my passport. When I got there, a clerk with lips like a fish stared at the passport, stared at me, opened and closed her mouth a few times, and said, "Looks just like you." I left the office in frustration and realized I was now in the only corner of France totally lacking in beauty. I took the first bus out of there. As I settled into my seat, I realized I was dreaming. "Please," I cried. "Please someone wake me up. I need to get out of this dream." Then I felt the lightest of touches on one cheek and opened my eyes, relieved to find myself in a bed I was sharing with four dogs.

Audrey was still missing. I called her cellphone again, and again I reached only voice mail. Barbara, Lois and I sighed our individual sighs and agreed we would keep everything going as if nothing had happened. With three of us working, the morning chores flew by. Lois then took charge of the phone. I concentrated on the emails. Barbara worked with a couple dogs that needed better leash behavior.

With emails out of the way, I blogged about Sam, a tall black lab mix.

Sam's sleek, healthy coat is a new look for him. A few months ago a lady out hiking in a state park came across this dog when he was close to death. Barely a skeleton, he wobbled as he walked. The lady took him home, fed him, and called the local shelter.

Shelter staff and volunteers spread the word. They had a dog that wasn't ready for adoption but really needed some help. After a week at the shelter, he was still very thin but was slowly gaining strength and weight. On the day we took him in, he was the last dog still waiting for rescue or adoption. He was a big, black dog. We named him Sam.

Sam was what we call a "needy" boy, always finding a way to be close to you. We figured he'd make a great family dog once he learned some basic obedience skills, including the inadvisability of taking food off the counter top. Ok, he has a good defense for his interest in food. But Sam, we want to call you a good boy. Don't you want that?

If Sam was a praying dog or even a wishing dog, his prayers and wishes were answered recently when a family asked to meet him. They immediately fell for his charms, and Sam went home to the kind of home he could probably not even imagine. That good.

Yesterday, we received a picture from Sam's new family. Smiling children bookended the tall, shiny, very healthy black dog.

And that's what we love about rescue.

I shut down the computer and stood up, stretching as if I were preparing for a run or a workout. Out the window by my desk I watched several dogs leaping over each other like hopscotching children. It was one of those summer days that cool off just enough to invite the appearance of airy little crocheted shawls draped over sundresses. I, however, was still in shorts and a t-shirt. I didn't own any airy shawl or even a sundress.

It was time to get on with finding Audrey. Barbara offered to make flyers and post them throughout town.

"If she shows up this afternoon and sees her picture all over town, she'll kill us," said Lois, and then "oops," embarrassed about using the "k" word. "Well at least we won't be putting her picture on a milk carton." We all giggled at the thought.

Lois said she would stay with the dogs and phone everyone she knew and ask them to call all their friends and acquaintances, sounding the alarm and hoping someone will know something or will have noticed something.

I took off to visit the oldest man in town, hoping he might help unlock some of the mysteries of the past that seemed now to be churning up trouble in the present.

Chapter 23

"You came to the right place. I know everything. I know everyone." Lars Sorensen's head bobbed up and down as I helped him back to his chair. He dropped into place and peered up at me through ragged white eyebrows. I tucked his lap blanket about him and wondered why old people seemed to have so much trouble staying warm.

"I thought you'd never ask. Everyone forgets about me, even my grandson. I could help him solve this town's mysteries. That's for sure."

I sat on the edge of the sofa, close enough to his chair that I wouldn't need to raise my voice to be heard. I was glad Chief Sorensen wasn't at home. I could ask more of my own questions, and the Chief's grandfather could talk more freely. At least I hoped that would be the case. I decided from the start that I would not treat him as an old person but rather as an expert on local history. My approach turned out to be the right one. I told him my suspicion that the past held the clues to what was happening today – to the death of two "Dog Ladies" and to the disappearance of another – Audrey.

He stared at his hands folded in his lap and pushed his lower lip out as if in deep thought.

"Yeeesssiree," he said finally, dragging out the word. "You could be right, could be wrong."

I encouraged him to go on. I asked if he could think of anything in Redbud history that might be significant.

He nodded and closed his eyes. For a moment I thought he'd fallen asleep.

"You're thinking about those ancestors of yours – Johannes and Karen – and all the stories about wealth and hidden treasure. Those stories have been causing trouble for a long time. Every year another grandchild or great grandchild or great great grandchild shows up trying to get to the truth. Been going on seems like forever."

I interrupted, impatient to keep him on track and wondering what he really knew.

"Do *you* know the truth? Did you know Karen and Johannes?"

He harrumphed. He actually harrumphed. I didn't know people actually did that. "I'm old, but I wasn't quite part of their generation. Johannes died in 1912; I was 7 or 8 years old. Karen had been dead several years by then. But I almost joined the family later when I met one of their granddaughters. Her name was Viola, and she looked a lot like you." He winked at me. I shaded my eyes from the rays of afternoon sun. I waited for him to begin his story.

"I loved that girl, but things didn't work out for us. But that Viola, she knew all the family secrets or thought she did, anyway. After her father died, Viola lived with Johannes and Karen for a time; her mother was teaching in a boys' boarding school. The usually quiet Karen opened up around Viola and told her things she'd never told any of her own children. I guess there's just something about growing old that makes you want to tell your stories."

"Anyway, Karen told Viola about her childhood on one of the Danish islands."

As he talked on, his words transported me to another place and time, a place where a little girl in a long skirt ran from her thatched roof home to a beach where she could look across the waters but wade into them only when no parents were nearby. She often stomped her feet in disgust and frustration as she watched little boys racing into the waters, splashing and shrieking. Why, she wondered, couldn't girls have as much fun as boys? On this day the little girl boldly pulled off her shoes, hiked up her skirts and stepped closer to the shore, finally edging her toes and then the rest of her feet into the foam edging her on. She sighed and stepped onward, finally submerging her feet in the water to just above her ankles. But then she had trouble keeping the gentle waves from wetting her skirt. She knew mama would be angry, so she stepped back onto the sand. The little girl returned to a bundle she'd left near a rock and pulled out a book. For two hours, she read about other worlds, other places, other lives.

The little girl was one of five children in a family with a good pedigree but little money. They had nobility in their lineage, or so they thought, and all the children grew up knowing they were meant for finer things but might need to settle for something less. A bright girl might someday become a governess for a wealthy family, and that is what happened to this little girl. That is what happened to Karen. One day she was a bookish child wishing she could play with the boys. Then some years later she was leading three young children through lessons in French, Danish literature, history and music. And everyone told her how fortunate she was to have such a position in an important house.

She did sometimes feel quite fine, a cut above the other servants. Her own parents had encouraged her to see herself that way, as someone who should be a princess or at least a countess if only the family hadn't lost its fortune. She wasn't sure how that could have happened. Perhaps someone stole it? The girl believed in her heart that she could as easily be the mistress as the governess. She walked straight and held her head high. And when the lord of the manor smiled her way, she smiled back. She felt superior to her mistress and wasn't surprised when smiles turned into touches and touches into caresses. He loved her. She glowed.

"I think I know what happens next," I interrupted. "We've all heard this story before. An older, powerful man seduces a young girl and then abandons her when she needs him most, when she becomes pregnant. Is that what happened?"

"Shhh," Lars Sorensen scolded, and continued his narrative.

The lord of the manor holds the young governess in his arms when she tells him she's pregnant. He kisses the top of her head and says they'll be together someday – just not now. He needs time. He has to think of his children. She must not tell anyone that he is the father. That would ruin everything. She should say it was someone who had visited the manor, someone whose name she couldn't remember, a charmer, a seducer. She must return to her parents and tell them that but never the truth. Not until they could be together. She pulled away. What would her parents think of her if she told them she was pregnant by a man whose name she couldn't remember?

Her mother screamed and called her names. Her father wept. For two days she slept in the barn, blanketed by straw, unwelcome in the house. Then her older brother persuaded her parents to forgive her and let her in. She might have been happier staying in the barn. Silence was her constant companion. She refused to name the father. Her parents refused to speak to her. And the baby's father was the most silent of all.

And still she believed he would come to her. She believed all throughout the pregnancy and the delivery of her daughter. She believed when her baby gurgled happily, and she believed when her baby cried through a fever. She believed when her daughter took her first steps.

Then one day as Karen and her daughter picked lilacs from the bushes in front of her parent's house, a horseman appeared with a message from the child's father, from the lord of the manor. His wife had learned about the baby born to her former governess. She was immediately suspicious and accused her husband. He decided it would be best if someone step forward and accept responsibility for Karen's child. He'd talked to one of his footmen, given him some land and enough to set up a business, and the footman had agreed to marry Karen and say he was the father. It's for the best. I'll never forget you. I'll always love you. Please believe that.

She no longer believed that. She no longer walked like a lady with her head high. She faded. She dipped her head as she walked past people in the village. But she did marry the footman, and she did let him tell people he was the child's father. As for the marriage? It was not for the best, as she would soon find out.

"It was not for the best," the old man repeated and then closed his eyes. His head dropped to his chest and he snored quietly.

"You've worn him out, it seems," said Chief Sorensen, as he stepped through the front door. Walking in behind him was Audrey.

I jumped to my feet. "Audrey! You're alive!" I'd feared the worst. I knew that now.

Both Audrey and Chief Sorensen laughed.

"Quite alive and quite embarrassed. It seems the entire county is out looking for me – maybe the entire state. Good heavens, someone has even put up signs. What am I? The dog that jumped the fence?"

"You didn't tell anyone where you were going! You didn't answer your phone! You just took off in a big hurry without a word." By then I'd stretched out both arms and was speaking to her as I'd never done before. I was angry. I was not going to let her get away with thinking her disappearance was no big deal." I lowered my voice. "We were all so worried."

89

With that, she held up both hands as if to surrender. In one smooth move, she closed the distance between us and wrapped her arms around me, patting the back of my head as I choked back tears. I tried to catch Chief Sorensen's eyes, to search out an explanation from him, but he looked away and turned instead to check on his father.

"I won't do this again," Audrey whispered.

Later that night, after Lois and Barbara had left and the dogs were put to bed, after Audrey had called a congregation of worried volunteers and reassured them that all was well, after I'd turned over in my mind the old man's story and wondered when I could go back for the next chapter, after I'd stilled the trembling in my hands, after Audrey had told me where she'd gone, only then did I understand just how frightened Audrey really was. Audrey is not a hugger. Her uncharacteristic embrace surprised me. I felt the warmth of reassurance, of affection. But I also felt a whisper of sadness, of farewell.

I understood she wouldn't disappear of her own free will. I knew that was all she could promise.

A soft tap on my bedroom door interrupted my thoughts. Audrey peeked in. "Got a minute?"

She sat on the edge of my bed and thought for a while. "I'm sorry I frightened you. I expected to be gone for less than a day. I've told you a little about my sister, but I don't think I told you about her son. His fingerprints were at the house along with those of my sister. When I learned that, I decided on a quick trip to Kansas City where he lived. I expected to find him and maybe my sister as well. But Charles wasn't at home. I spent the rest of my time there trying to find him without success. Much of that time I was just sitting on a bus bench near where he lived. Then earlier today no other than Chief Sorensen sat down next to me on that bench."

There's more, isn't there? "

She nodded abruptly. "I also suspected Charles could be the murderer. And now that he seems to be somewhere other than his own home, I'm even more worried. "

"Is he the reason your sister changed her name and disappeared into a new life? She was hiding from him?"

90

She was afraid and ashamed. Charles was never quite right, and as he grew older his behavior became worse. But he could be very charming. He could fool. He fooled the young woman who married him."

"I take it they are not together anymore."

"No, but not from divorce. Ellie died mysteriously. Charles said he came home one day to find her dead. Cause of death was an overdose of phenobarbital."

"Oh!" I gasped.

"Police finally ruled it a suicide but not before my sister – her name is Jessica -- told police of her suspicions – that her own son had murdered his wife. You see it wasn't the first time Charles had been a suspect in a murder. He was only 14 when police questioned him about the murder of one of his classmates. Someone had seen him with the victim that day, but the witness later retracted his story and police didn't find the murder weapon. Charles went free.

"But Jessica knew, right?"

"Not only did she know, but I think she helped him get rid of the knife that was probably the murder weapon. He'd convinced her he hadn't meant to kill the other boy, only frighten him. As his mother, she thought she was doing the right thing and that he would grow up to be a good person."

I could see where this story was going, and Audrey's words confirmed it. Jessica saw more and more violent behavior from her charming son. Every time she heard of a murder or suspicious death, she wondered if Charles might be responsible. She almost warned the young woman when she became engaged to Charles. But she held back. Maybe. Maybe everything would be ok. Maybe Charles was different now that he had found someone to love.

Audrey continued, "But when she learned of the death of Charles' wife, Jessica could stay silent no more. She knew her son was a danger to others. When the story broke in the media, Jessica became known as 'the mother who turned in her son.' When police refused to charge Charles with murder, some in the media called her 'the mother who accused her innocent son of murder.'"

The poor woman, I thought. How terrible to know you've raised a murderer. How even more terrible to know that if you'd spoken up earlier, if you hadn't helped cover up the earlier crime, a young woman might still be alive.

"I think I told you already that Jessica and I had an uncomfortable relationship. We'd had a falling out many years ago. During the problems with Charles, I talked to her a few times, offering support, but she turned me away. I know she was ashamed and afraid. She moved to New York City because she hoped Charles wouldn't follow her there. But one day she saw him on the street, watching her. She called me once to say she was receiving threatening phone calls and notes. She'd said she was thinking about changing her name and moving somewhere Charles couldn't find her

"Then 911. Jessica was at work in a brokerage firm. Although some co-workers had noticed her on the stairs, no one saw her again after that day. Even I didn't know the truth for some time. I guess she believed that as long as Charles thought she was dead, she was safe. So on that day she just took off."

Audrey said many years passed before she heard from Jessica, a surprise call from a throwaway cellphone. After that, an occasional call just to touch base. In the meantime, Audrey had moved from California to Redbud. One day Charles showed up at Audrey's door acting all mysterious. He said he was looking for his mother and that he knew she was still alive. Audrey tried to convince him Jessica was gone, but Charles only laughed.

"From time to time I'd see Charles' face in a crowd – sometimes at an adoption event, sometimes in a restaurant. Sometimes I thought I recognized Jessica too. Maybe she was keeping an eye on me too for some reason."

One day Carl and Bella told Audrey about a man who'd come in asking about her. Their description of the man matched that of Charles. The man even left his Kansas City address."

I thought that Jessica must have been as lonely as she was frightened. Why else would she decide to show up here? I shared this question with Audrey.

92

Audrey said that when she heard Carl and Bella talking about Goldie La Chien, she knew it was her sister's way of letting her know she was here. She also knew Jessica would never be safe here since Charles was watching and waiting.

Audrey fell backwards onto the bed with her hands behind her head. She stared at the ceiling. "I wish I'd had a chance to speak to my sister. We'd never gotten along that well. I was hoping we could put that behind us and start over."

She looked up at me. "I'd actually dreaded going to see her. I didn't know what to expect. She was always so angry at everything and everyone and especially at me. She was furious when I married Eric. She wanted me to step aside and let her have a chance with him. What she didn't understand was that she never had a chance with Eric. He didn't even like her."

"Were you and Eric happy together?"

"Oh yes. Very. But he died when he was only 35 of what the doctors called an undetected heart disease. One day he was fine and then..." She waved a hand to one side. "Gone."

I paused before asking my next question.

What about Jessica? Who is Charles' father?"

"Jessica married a veterinarian. How ironic. I was the one who loved animals, but she was the one to marry a veterinarian. They lasted about two years together. They were in the midst of a nasty divorce when he died in an auto accident."

Audrey sat up and put her hands on her knees. "At times I felt sorry for Charles. It couldn't have been easy having Jessica as a mother. In many ways, they were a lot of alike. Both could be charming when it suited them. Both had their dark sides. But with Charles, it seems the dark side took over."

Audrey stood up to leave, softly closing the door behind her. Then a couple seconds later, she pushed the door open a crack and looked back in.

"I've told all this to Chief Sorensen. He'll look into it. Maybe we should forget all this for a while. How would you like to go to a dog auction? Maybe we could save a few dogs from spending the rest of their days breeding too many puppies."

A dog auction?

Chapter 24

The next day we looked online at a list of dogs going up for auction in a Missouri auction house. We printed out the list and checked off those that we might want to bid on. Audrey said she couldn't spend much money but hoped we'd come home with a few. She circled information on the two oldest dogs at the auction. "They deserve a few years as pets," she said. Then she underlined a few female dogs that were five or six years-- "a good time to retire from breeding. They should have most of their lives ahead of them." Then she sighed and added that "sometimes a dog just calls to us and we can't say no."

Audrey warned me that dog auctions can be disturbing, but neither of us seemed anything but excited as we planned for our four-hour drive to the auction location. Barbara and Lois would take care of things while we were gone. I even went out and bought a few new items of clothing – pants, shirts, and a cardigan sweater in case autumn slipped in unannounced.

The best part is that we didn't have time to think about much else. We didn't have time to be sad or afraid. Granted, I'd hoped to visit Chief Sorensen and tag along with his investigation. And true, I was most anxious to visit the Chief's grandfather again to hear more of his story.

But for now I was ready for a new kind of rescue.

We left home at 5 a.m., slipping away from Redbud in the dark. We waved at Lois and Barbara as they pulled into the driveway we'd just pulled out of. From a thermos of coffee, I poured us both a cup. As we drove, Audrey filled me in on proper auction behavior. We wouldn't be the only rescuers there, but most of the bidders would be breeders looking for new dogs to add to their kennels. Some of the breeders resented rescuers.

"Just mind your manners and don't use the words 'puppy mill.' They really hate being called puppy millers. I can understand that with some of the better breeders, but all the same, many deserve the title. Just don't use it today. And don't make comments about how sad the dogs look even if they do look sad. Don't get misty-eyed or indignant.

Just blend in. Don't pretend to be a breeder but don't advertise the fact that you're part of a rescue group."

I promised to behave and for a long time we drove on in companionable silence. I studied our printout and made a few notes of my own. And I also thought about my former life in St. Louis and the things I'd lost there. I hadn't anticipated how I might feel retracing the route that had been my escape from all that had happened. I didn't want to think of my husband or my child or that unspeakably tragic day when everything spiraled out of control. I didn't want to remember my job or my house or anything else that belonged to that other life, that other me. As we crossed into Missouri, I felt like I couldn't breathe properly. I bowed my head and closed my eyes, trying to disappear into myself. Audrey noticed and began lecturing me some more about puppy mills, pet overpopulation, and a long list of dog diseases. I forced myself to listen and eventually I opened my eyes and breathed easier.

"I know what happened to you, or at least I know what I could find online. I'm so sorry." Audrey peered at me without turning her head. I bit into my lower lip. Better a bruised lip that a loose tear.

"I know you don't want to talk about it. I don't think I would either. But please know that you're not alone."

For Audrey, the brief speech was unusually soft. I should have known she would check me out. I mean, who just opens the door to a complete stranger? I could have been anyone... anything. But still, I had hoped I was free in Redbud, free from my past, free from my secrets, free from my shame. I could only nod, accepting her sympathy, a sentiment I'd learned to despise.

Thank God, her voice quickly turned from soft to gruff, "Of course, I haven't shared what I know with anyone else. I suspect Chief Sorensen might have checked you out, though."

So did I. I'd seen that much in his eyes.

Both of us seemed uncomfortable for a few minutes, stiff and silent. Finally, Audrey started in again on dog auctions and puppy mills, talking rapidly as she rattled off both facts and opinions.

I learned that although most people have never heard of dog auctions, you can find several every month in Missouri alone. Breeders come to sell off some of the dogs they no longer need while at the same time looking for new dogs and new breeds to purchase. Rescuers come to purchase as many dogs as possible, saving them from spending their entire lives having puppies with every new heat cycle. A few "flippers" buy dogs at auctions and then turn around and sell them the next day for a profit – without providing any veterinary care first. And sometimes people are there to find a pet for themselves.

As we drove on, Audrey noted that the worst breeders kept their dogs confined in cages 24/7. And the worst of the worst barely cleaned those cages, so the dogs slept in their own urine and feces. When released from their cages, some of these dogs could barely walk. Grass terrified them, and many shrank from human touch. Audrey added that not all commercial breeders are bad. "I've known some breeders who made sure their dogs got enough exercise and good care, some who made sure their dogs lived in clean, climate-controlled facilities. Some of them do love their animals." But with a huff, she added, "But for many of them, maybe most of them, their dogs are just another money crop."

I napped for a while and woke as we pulled into a gravel lot next to a long low building. We pulled in between two pickups and stepped out into a warm but breezy morning, stretched a bit, and followed two men in overalls into the building. I saw bleachers on two sides and several rows of chairs in front of a low barrier that separated the audience from the sales area.

"That's where they bring the dogs out," Audrey pointed. "And the auctioneer is always up there." I looked up at an elevated platform overlooking the long table, where I guessed we'd see the dogs as they were being auctioned off. I claimed two seats down front while Audrey stood in a short line to claim her bidding card and the final list of dogs being auctioned. Several people already occupied spots on the chairs and bleachers, but most seemed to be disappearing through a door leading to another room. Each time the door opened, the barking from within spilled out. Soon Audrey and I were squeezing down crowded aisles, peeking in cages and writing notes on our lists. I soon saw the differences between dogs. Some huddled in the backs of their cages. Others stepped forward and sniffed our hands. Some even wagged their tails and a few

97

their entire bodies. All wore numbered tags dangling from string collars. Some "called" to us, to use Audrey's word. I circled #8 and #88 as particular favorites.

"It all depends on how high the bids go," Audrey whispered. "I can't and won't bid much, but sometimes we get lucky. "Audrey flipped past a couple pages on her list and found the listings for several older females. She circled their numbers, writing so hard she split the paper. "I'd love to retire these girls."

As we reached the end of one row, a large woman with blazing red hair grabbed Audrey's arm and yanked her aside. At first I feared the woman might be a breeder Audrey had offended and who was now ready to exact vengeance. I stepped backwards and almost knocked over a cage. "Hey!" someone yelled, and I turned to apologize. At the same time I heard the woman hissing at Audrey. "I need to talk to you before you leave. Not now or they'll think we're conspiring to fix prices. But it's urgent. You need to know this!"

With that, the large woman marched stoutly away down the aisle we'd just left. Audrey pursed her lips and looked my way. One shoulder went up. Who knows?

We returned to our seats just as the auctioneer took his place and began barking out the rules of the auction. Several persons hustled out from the dog area to find seats. Someone latched the door behind them, making sure no one could wander back there during the auction.

And so we began.

Several young people carried out six Chihuahuas and held them in place on the table. The auctioneer rattled and rumbled and sometimes mumbled while two spotters yelped and pointed at each new bidder. Finally the bidding stopped, and the winner selected two of the Chihuahuas. Then the bidding started over again.

Audrey and I sat silently and shook our heads as the bids reached new highs on several fluffy Shih Tzu puppies. Finally I sat up straight because #8, an older blue merle sheltie now stared directly at me from where she was on the auction table. I wanted her but waited until the auctioneer failed to attract a bidder at $100 and then at $50 and finally dropped the starting price down to $25. Then I lifted Audrey's bidding

98

card. Next thing I knew two other bidders jumped in at $30 and then at $50. But suddenly the bidding stopped and the auctioneer pointed at me. "We got her," I said to Audrey, beaming.

Audrey smiled back. "Sometimes we get lucky. Must not have been any sheltie people here today." She slapped me on the back. I'd already renamed my new rescue dog Blue Lady.

The auction burned on, with occasional bidding battles, especially for certain "hot" breeds, such as the French Bulldogs that went for $800 and more. Eventually, Audrey won the bid for a couple Pomeranians and a Yorkshire terrier – older females that she bought for $30 and $40. Then a 5-year-old Yorkshire terrier came up for auction. Information on our bid sheet said she'd had a C-section with her last litter. Audrey's fingers stroked her bid card. I knew she wouldn't let this lady go to a breeder.

"Don't worry about the C-section," the auctioneer said. "All you need to do is get one more litter from her and you'll make your money back and a good bit more."

Audrey now clutched her bid card, hissing for my ears only. "It's totally irresponsible to breed a dog that's had a C-section. The uterus could rupture."

A few minutes later, this little dog was ours, but Audrey had spent the rest of our money getting her. "It was worth it," Audrey muttered, not wanting to hear that she'd gone ridiculously high because she'd let her emotions and her anger carry her away. She wouldn't hear that from me. I was enjoying the fizz rushing from my toes to my head. "Let's call her Lucy," I said. It's only one letter away from Lucky, and thanks to us, that's just what she is today. Lucky. Audrey just smiled.

With all our funds gone, we pushed back our chairs and walked back to the counter where we paid and picked up our paperwork. Then we left the building to move our van to another door where we could claim and load up our purchases.

Just as we walked out with our paperwork, Audrey lurched forward and nearly toppled as the large woman with the blazing red hair blasted through the door behind us, unable to stop fast enough to avoid a collision. I jumped aside just in time.

"Jeez, Diane," Audrey made a show of dusting off her pants even though she hadn't fallen. "I didn't forget about you." Then she introduced me to "another of us dog ladies. This is Diane with Pets for You Rescue. She might look a little wild, but she's one of the sane ones. Diane, meet one of my new recruits."

Diane reached out a plump hand and pumped mine, then turned to Audrey and grabbed the front of her shirt.

"Another Dog Lady is dead. Murdered!"

Another dog lady is dead? Murdered? I leaned in to hear the rest because Diane was bent almost head to head with Audrey, spitting out the horrible news.

Another dog lady dead! Murdered! The word kept spinning through my head.

Remember Pat Arnold?"

"Who doesn't? That woman is an embarrassment to dog rescue and maybe even to the human race. I wanted her out of dog rescue, but are you saying she's dead?

"Murdered! Oh for God's sake, what's going on? First Kansas. Now Missouri."

Diane must not have heard about Lydia Harrison in Nebraska or the message sent to the television stations.

Audrey closed her eyes for a moment. "No. Please no. Not another. " Her face had gone pale.

"Do they have a suspect?" I asked.

Diane shook her head. "They think she was poisoned, but they're still investigating. Some of us have been picking up her dogs. The poor things. I don't like to speak ill of the dead, but most of Pat's dogs were in bad shape, living in filth. I hate to even claim her as a rescue person."

But there it is, I thought. Another Dog Lady is dead.

Audrey looked across the parking lot as if scanning for a suspect. "The way Pat lived, I know she had plenty of enemies. Maybe one of them got to her. Maybe she owed money to the wrong person. Her death might not have anything to do with dog rescue."

"Or it might," answered Diane.

We all closed our mouths and looked around.

"Or it might," repeated Audrey.

Another Dog Lady is dead! The words wouldn't leave my head. Murdered!

Finally, Audrey broke away. "We need to load up." She moved towards our van and Diane towards the door to the auction house. Then both stopped, turned, faced each other again and in unison uttered the same words.

"Be careful."

Chapter 25

I'm meeting someone for dinner but have lost the address of the restaurant. I see myself and another person walking down a wide road with hundreds of other people walking in both directions. No automobiles. Just people walking. I'm wearing a dress and a light blue full-length coat. Everyone else wears short sleeves, no coats. I stop at what I think is a park but which turns out to be an office building. I try to call for directions but can't remember how to use my cellphone. I'm late. I know I'm late. The person with me is tapping her toe. Tap, Tap, Tap. She doesn't speak, but I know she wants me to hurry. I'm starting to cry. What's wrong with my smart phone? What's wrong with me? If Paul were here, he'd know what to do. But Paul isn't here, and I don't know what to do.

I wake up, startled and relieved. It was only a dream. Sometimes I think psychiatrists have such a great job. They can listen to people's dreams and make obvious connections. I can make the same connections myself – the loss, the confusion. I just don't know what to do with what I know. Maybe that's where the shrinks would shine if they'd say more than "go on." Or maybe "go on" is their advice and not meant as just a prompt to keep talking. Life goes on and so must you.

This is the first dream I've had in the almost two weeks since the dog auction. I don't want to think about Paul or about what happened to him and to me and to our baby. That old feeling overcomes me. I close my eyes and feel myself floating away until the ceiling stops my flight. Below me are five dogs on my bed – Faith, Scarlett, two new beagles named Fern and Thistle, and a dog from the auction – the blue merle sheltie I'd named Blue Lady.

I concentrate on the dogs. That's what Audrey would say. Don't worry about dreams. Worry about dogs. Don't worry about the past or the future. Just take care of the dogs. I open my eyes and I'm back on the bed where I belong with four dogs arranged around me like petals around a stem. I run my fingers through the thick fur around Blue Lady's neck. She licks my ear. She's a sweet dog and only a little shy. She wants to be friends. I've bathed her twice and she's looking much better, but her white ruff is still stained yellow from sleeping in her own urine at the puppy mill. Two of the other dogs from the auction are still so terrified they won't let us near them. Kati, the C-section dog Audrey spent too much for, nearly died during spay surgery. The vet said the breeder probably did the C-section without anesthesia and botched the job. That made the spay surgery more complicated and lengthy. Fortunately, the little dog pulled through and is now our miracle dog. Defying all odds, she's pretty much a normal dog. She loves everyone and climbs onto any available lap. We've already collected three application for her and expect more. We'll find her a great new home. She would almost certainly have died without our help.

We've been busy at Redbud Area Dog Rescue with dogs coming in and others finding forever homes. And....

And Oh My God! I bolt straight up. Now fully awake, I remember that we've all had more on our minds the past weeks than dogs or any of our own sad pasts. Someone was killing dog ladies? How ridiculous is that? And how frightening. One of the nearby dailies ran a headline across the length of the page: "Who is killing the Dog Ladies?" Suddenly dog ladies and dog rescue groups were big news.

Since returning from the dog auction, detectives from three different states have knocked on our door. Our phone rings constantly with panicky calls from others in the dog rescue community. Our volunteers are scared and locking their doors at night, something they've never felt necessary before. Chief Sorensen has been here several times. Since hearing about the murder of Pat Arnold in Missouri, we've learned of three other murders in other states – all of women running dog rescue organizations. Except for Pat Arnold, all the women ran respectable organizations with all the proper licenses and tax-exempt status. Pat Arnold seemed to be the only disreputable dog lady, more hoarder than rescuer. Some thought her murder might not be connected to the others. Audrey said Pat Arnold owed a lot of people money, including her.

What's the strange part? All the victims had one thing in common. They all knew Audrey.

This country, I now know is littered with dog ladies who rescue dogs either on their own or as part of a dog rescue organization. Audrey is the preeminent dog lady here, but almost every county has at least one woman with that title. Some are sophisticated and well-educated. Some flunked out of high school and wouldn't know a symphony from a kitchen sink. Some are shy and withdrawn. Others have voices like foghorns and personalities to match. Many know each other and are friends. Many others know each other and are definitely not friends. Rescue people often disagree about how best to run a dog rescue business. When they're not complaining about breeders and irresponsible pet owners, they're complaining about each other. All of which complicates the investigation, Chief Sorensen patiently explained one evening as he sat in our living room with his head in his hands, his elbows on his knees.

"The detectives I've met with no longer think it's strange that someone is killing the dog ladies," he said, looking up at Audrey through his fingers. "They're wondering why it took so long."

Audrey stiffened just a little. This was not the time for humor, but I saw one corner of her mouth twitch. Then she pulled herself back into serious mode. "Since these murders, we're all drawing together, closing ranks. All our disagreements seem unimportant now. We're scared and we're sticking together."

"How many of you are sticking together?" Chief Sorensen lifted his head from his hands and sat up straight in his chair.

Audrey said she knew about 50 other dog ladies, either personally or through email groups or Facebook.

"Only 50?"

"That's still quite a few," I added.

"But that's out of several thousand nationwide."

Chief Sorensen lifted his long frame out of his chair. "So what are the odds that you would know all of the murdered dog ladies?"

Audrey merely looked at him.

"You're the key, Audrey. You're the one thing linking all of these murders. Someone isn't just killing Dog Ladies. Someone is killing Dog Ladies you know. These outstate detectives aren't just stopping by to chat because they like you so much. "

No, I thought, they're stopping by because of Audrey's sister Jessica and her nephew Charles. Jessica was still missing. She hadn't tried to contact Audrey. Charles also was missing. He hadn't returned to his Kansas City home since the murder in Redbud.

I wondered if some of the detectives suspected Audrey. Maybe they thought she knew the whereabouts of her sister and nephew. Could they possible think she was an accomplice? That just didn't make sense. It would be like suspecting Mother Teresa of mass murder. What motive would Audrey have for killing other dog ladies? None. Maybe the detectives should spend their time scoping out the puppy millers. They were the ones who hated the dog ladies.

That was my thinking. If it wasn't Audrey's nephew behind this, it must be a crazed puppy miller. If Old Man Schmidt hadn't been past 80, I would have suspected him.

I knew what Audrey believed, and I think Chief Sorensen felt the same way. The killer wanted Audrey but was sending her a warning with each new murder, building the terror. I looked at her face and knew I was right. She was afraid. She knew she was the target – the main target. But was she next?

Chief Sorensen put an arm around Audrey's shoulders and talked softly. "Call anytime you think of something that might help us stop this person."

"And be careful." Chief Sorensen took in both of us with those final words before he excused himself and walked out the door.

I needed to meet with him again. Maybe I could help. I also wanted to pay another visit to his grandfather to hear more about my ancestors. I still sensed a connection between these murders and something in the distant past. Call me crazy because I probably am. But I feel a connection. I'm just not dumb enough to mention it.

All of this went through my mind as I pushed the dogs off my bed and got out of bed. I pulled on my new pair of jeans and a long sleeved t-shirt. Fall was sneaking into our lives to replace the sizzle and sweat of summer. A few minutes later, I was out in the kitchen, ready to help Audrey feed the dogs.

Chapter 26

I'm still not a dog person, but dogs are now so much a part of my life that it no longer matters what I think I am. I wake up with dogs and I go to sleep with them. I clean up after them without complaint and I've even learned a few training tricks. I no longer swear when I step in poo. I just scrape it off and get on with my day.

Audrey says she'll take care of the emails this morning, so I wash dishes and answer the phone. When the phone stops ringing for a while, I walk over to Audrey and peer over her shoulder at the computer. She's on Facebook, which is full of postings from other dog rescue groups. Everyone is worried about the murders. And why not?

"Does anyone say anything useful?

Audrey dumps a small dog off her lap and turns to look up at me. "No. Mainly, they're all mystified. They can't imagine why anyone would want to murder harmless women who rescue dogs."

"Harmless?" I smile. "I wouldn't want to face an army of Dog Ladies who thought I'd mistreated an animal."

"In that case, maybe we need to sharpen our fangs a little more. We're not nearly scary enough since the mistreatment of animals goes on." As she signed off Facebook and onto email, Audrey repeated her concern about not seeing her sister in Redbud. "I just wish I'd been able to talk to her. Oh, I know we never did get along. But I did stick by her during all the trouble with her son even if she didn't want my help. Truth is I actually dreaded seeing her again. I thought she was looking for some sort of show down."

She remained quiet for a while as she clicked through emails. "But maybe if we'd actually talked, things would have been different."

I thought for a moment of the sharply dressed body I'd found in the doorway of our ancestor's home. "What about Lydia Harrison? She was researching the Jensen family. She and Jessica knew each other. Lydia was actually moving here. Where does she fit in?"

Audrey looked up. "It took me a while, but I finally remembered Lydia. We met at a conference in New York City a few years back. She's even on one of my email lists. Of course, I never knew we were distant cousins."

"But how did she and Jessica know each other?"

"Chief Sorensen is working on that question. He thinks they might have met through a genealogy group and found out they were researching the same family. That might explain why they both ended up here in Redbud."

Lydia was a Dog Lady of sorts, but she dealt more with fundraising and administration. That would explain why she didn't really look like a Dog Lady." Audrey laughed and swept one hand from her head to her foot, pointing out corkscrew curls, torn-t-shirt, baggy pants, and mud-caked boots.

"Was Jessica really a stock broker before 911?"

"She was. And although New York City is a plenty big city, she and Lydia might even have met while they were both living there.

"How well did you know your sister's son?"

"Not at all, but like I said, I felt sorry for him at times. Life couldn't have been easy for him with my sister as his mother. But plenty of children grow up with imperfect parents and don't turn into monsters."

I remembered that in my early days as a newspaper reporter, I'd been surprised to find out that most violent crime was a family affair. That's why murders were usually so easy to solve.

Audrey scrolled through her emails. With practiced haste, she told several emailers that she didn't have room for their dogs but suggested they check back next week. She sent a glowing description of one of our dogs to someone asking advice on which dog to adopt. She attached an application to several emails from people interested in various dogs, including Kati, the C-section dog. She deleted the junk and several emails telling her about dogs in Georgia and Mississippi. "We don't need to go that far. We still have plenty of dogs in need close to home. If that ever changes, then I'll start looking at those long distance dogs. It might happen someday, but it hasn't happened yet."

Audrey stopped then at an email with the headline "To Aunt Audrey." She opened it and read, "I understand you are looking for me. Really?"

Chapter 27

That afternoon I backed out of the driveway and pulled away for a quick trip to Chief Sorensen's home. I decided to drop by my ancestor's home on the way. Without a key, I couldn't get into the house, so I walked down towards the pond where several ducks paddling silently. I found a wooden bench where I could look out over the lake and imagine what life would have been like here more than a hundred years ago. Did the bench go back that far? Probably not. Someone had added it as a peaceful spot for relaxing or reading a book.

I closed my eyes and wondered if Karen and Johannes had also looked out over this same pond and sighed on a late summer day, enjoying the fading of the sweltering Nebraska summer. Did chickens scurry loose through the yard? Did Karen tend a large vegetable garden? Where did Johannes house the farm animals? And where did those animals graze? What crops did he raise? Were they happy together? And what of the children? Was one of the children more like Audrey's sister than like Audrey? Was one of them something like me? Was one like Carl? Or Audrey's nephew?

I was sitting near the spot where I'd seen Carl swaying his metal detector slowly over the ground. Walking through tall grass near the lake's edge, I noticed an area where the ground had been disturbed. I poked at it awhile with a stick, saw nothing unusual and turned to leave. Then just past the disturbed area I saw something catch the light. I leaned over, brushed some fallen branches aside, and picked up what looked like a long-lost coin. I hoped to find a date on it, so I rubbed some of the dirt away on my jeans and looked at it again. This was no penny, no nickel, no dime, no quarter. No silver dollar either. This coin was something I'd never seen before: a gold coin.

I'll bet this is worth something, I thought. Maybe I will buy some new clothes.

I tucked the coin in my pocket and strode back towards my car. A short time later I knocked on Chief Sorensen's door, and this time he was at home.

"I just learned something interesting from Audrey," I said as he opened the door for me.

"Something I don't already know?"

"Lydia and her sister didn't get along. Did you know that? And Lydia's sister wasn't a very nice person. Her son must have learned at her knee."

"Now that doesn't surprise me," he said.

"But did she also tell you she was afraid her sister was here for a show down of sorts and she'd been avoiding her? And did she tell you she remembered meeting Lydia Harrison? And are you really looking for a link between Lydia and Audrey's sister Jessica? And how much did she really tell you about her nephew Charles. Did she tell you how charming he can be?"

For a second I thought he was about to put his hands over his ears.

I realized I was talking too fast.

He smiled. "What I didn't know I suspected. But I think I need to sit on Audrey a little more. I think she knows things she doesn't realize she knows, things that could break this case open."

He tapped his head as if tipping a hat and said he needed to get back to work and also meet with Audrey again.

The Chief nodded at his grandfather. "Talk to him for a while. He likes you."

I watched him stride towards his car, then turned to smile at Lars Sorensen. The old man smiled back.

"You're here for more of the story."

And he picked up where he'd left off, with the fact that Karen's marriage to her lover's footman was "not a good thing."

"How do you know that?" I interrupted him. "Who would really know?"

"That's what the lovely Viola told me. Maybe she just imagined some things—you know, filled in the blanks with her own stories of what made sense to her. But Karen did leave Denmark a few years after her marriage, leaving her daughter and a new baby behind. As for the husband, nobody knows."

110

That much I knew from my own research. Karen left two children behind with her brother and immigrated to America, settling first in Council Bluffs, Iowa. But I was never able to find anything about her first husband other than the record of their marriage. Did he die? Did he run off? Did he abandon Karen and her children? Or did Karen leave him, sneaking away in the night to escape an abusive husband? Did they divorce? Was that even possible in the 1870s? I shot off my questions as the old man folded his hands in his lap and waited for me to finish.

"Something happened and it must have been bad. That much Viola learned from her talks with her grandmother. Something that would make a mother leave her children behind, not knowing if she'd ever see them again."

In my mind, I imagined several possibilities and tried them out on the old man. I already had a picture of Karen as someone capable of both recklessness and passion and maybe a little selfishness. She'd wanted a life of status and wealth. She found herself in a loveless match with a man she thought was beneath her. What could she do to escape the dismal future that stretched before her? Maybe she answered the siren call of the new world. For her time, she was independent and unwilling to settle for traditions she found ridiculous. She could be anything in America. No one would know her past. She was still young enough and beautiful enough to attract a good husband.

"But what would she do about the husband she already had? This was the question Viola and I discussed for hours on end. We arrived at a lot of crazy ideas, but only a couple that worked."

"So Karen never told Viola the whole truth?"

"No, Karen only said she had to leave Denmark in a hurry. She said she had no choice. That was something Viola remembered perfectly. She said she had no choice. Karen also said a friend helped her escape by finding her a governess job with a wealthy family immigrating to America. Karen used the word 'escape.' Viola was sure of that."

I stood up and began pacing. I called it my "thinking walk," something I'd employed during my newspaper days even in the news room. My "walks" amused my coworkers or annoyed them. I was never sure which. "There she goes again," someone would say. "Judy's thinking. Watch out."

I paced back and forth from front door to dining room window, stopping in front of the old man whenever I had something to say. His eyes followed my movements; his eyes laughed.

I had trouble imagining that she just packed her bag one day, dropped off the kids at her brother's, and caught a ship to the New World. I did know that a single woman with children could not have immigrated to America then. Not unless she had a husband waiting for her there.

So what did that leave? I stopped and looked at the old man, twisting my hands in front of me. "I keep thinking about the words 'hurry' and 'escape.' Makes me think he was beating her and she had to get away from him before he killed her or the children. But if that were the case, why would she leave the children behind in the same village where her husband could easily find them and maybe insist on taking them home with him, perhaps as a way of luring her back home – if he wanted her back?"

"Yes, why would she leave her children? Did she care more about her own safety than about theirs? Could she have been that selfish?" The old man paused for emphasis before the line I was sure to understand. "Would any woman leave her babies? Knowing she might never see them again?"

A single sob escaped. I turned it into a cough. I knew the answer. When I'd kissed my own baby for the last time, I expected to see him again that evening and to know him for the rest of my life.

"He wasn't alive when she left," I said.

He nodded. "That's what Viola and I decided."

"But why the hurry? Why the escape? If he'd died from disease or accident, why hadn't she told Viola that when she was telling her so much else?"

We looked at each other. An image appeared in my head as if on a screen. Screaming. Anger. The man shoves the woman against the wall and draws back his fist. A toddler screams in the corner. An infant wails from a crib. The woman ducks and falls near the fireplace. The man lashes out with his foot. She twists in pain and her hand falls on the

112

fireplace poker. Crab walking backwards, she pulls the poker behind her, boosts herself up and swings the poker at the head of the man lunging her way. He drops.

"Viola and I figured that was the sort of thing Karen would never want anyone to know. She'd killed her husband. Not intentionally. But she killed him all the same."

"But did it really happen that way?"

"We'll never know. "

Granted, I'd never been able to find any record of the death of Karen's first husband. I knew that if Karen had killed her husband, she probably would have been charged with murder. Would she have escaped prison? There's that word "escape" again. What would she have done?

Putting myself in her position, I imagine I would have asked for help. She might have turned to her brother or maybe to her ex-lover, the lord of the manor. It might have been easy to take the body out on a boat and dump it into the Baltic Sea. Then they could fabricate a story about how he had just not come home one day. He's been threatening to leave her for a long time. She would be an object of pity but would not be charged with murder.

The old man yawned. I knew our session was almost over. I asked, "Couldn't she have kept up the charade forever and stayed where she was? Why did she leave in a hurry?"

He shrugged. Maybe a body washed up on the shore. Maybe his relatives started asking questions. Maybe she couldn't live with his ghost. Things were closing in on her, and she asked for help again.

"So her ex-lover found her a job that would take her to America. And her brother took the children. She came to America and met Johannes Jensen."

"Ah yes, and she met Johannes. But that's for another day. "

I picked up my purse and patted him on the arm. "Thank you." Then I remembered the other thing I wanted to ask him about. I slipped my hand into my pocket and pulled out the gold coin.

"I found this out at the old homestead."

His eyes lit up and he reached for it, bringing it close to his eyes as he fingered it.

"I haven't seen one of these in a very long time. Not since I was a boy."

Chapter 28

Carl twisted the coin in front of his eyes, squinting to read the date.

"1888. You've found a Liberty five dollar gold coin. It's worth a lot more than five dollars today – at least $250. With the right date and in pristine condition, a coin like this could bring a thousand or more.

After leaving Chief Sorensen's, I'd headed for Bella's to share my find with Carl, who was the one person who probably had a few just like this.

"This is what you were looking for with your metal detector, right? I found it near where you were swinging your stick about"

He nodded as he continued to study my coin. "I found a few that day near the pond. The detector started ticking, and I dug away for a few minutes and uncovered the coins. I wonder if I dropped one of them."

"Well, it's mine now," I said, snatching the coin from his fingers. "How many of these have you found out there?"

"Only a few, but I keep thinking there must be a cache somewhere. The few I've found seem more like coins that slipped through a hole in someone's pocket. I sure would like to find several hundred gold coins."

Wouldn't we all, I thought, as I looked around the restaurant. It was late afternoon. Most of the tables were empty, but at one end of the restaurant, teenagers had pulled together two tables and were now reliving their school day over pie and soda. Laughter erupted regularly, punctuating the end of most sentences.

"You've really brought something nice to this town," I said. "Bella's is even popular with young people."

Carl beamed, or I thought he did. One hand went to his mouth, as if to smooth down his mustache, so I couldn't be sure of a smile. I still thought of him as The Walrus and Bella as The Words. "The young people discovered us early last years. Now we see some of them almost every day after the high school lets out. And once they head for home – with their appetites ruined– we start seeing the senior citizens in for early dinner, followed by younger locals and families, and even later by couples who've driven in from Omaha. Redbud's been good for us, too."

Since the evening when I learned about Carl and Bella's tragic loss, I've felt close to both of them. Several times I nearly told one or the other about what had happened to me. But always at the last moment, my throat closed and I couldn't talk. Carl began chatting again about gold coins and other buried treasures. He said something that caught my attention. Many of the Old West gamblers insisted on payment in gold coins. "Maybe they liked the way it jingled," he laughed.

"Carl!" I reached out and touched his hand. "Did I tell you about the old newspaper clipping Chief Sorensen showed me? "

I told him about the one line near the close of an article about gamblers, the line about Jos the Dane, who always won big on the rare occasions when he sat down to play. Carl looked at me with growing Interest.

"Johannes Jensen always signed his name 'Jos'!"

Carl stood up, almost knocking over his chair. "That's it! That must be it! Our great great or however great he was grandfather won big at the gambling tables of the Old West."

"And buried coins so his ancestors would find them," I said. But that didn't really make sense to me as I said it, and I could tell by Carl's drooping shoulders and the way he slid back into his chair, that it didn't sound right to him, either."

"I can believe he could have been a gambler, and a gifted one at that. But why wouldn't he need the money to support his farm and family? The gambling money probably just kept things going. Why would he hide a fortune in gold coins?"

"The coins we found might be a few he lost. Maybe that's all there is."

But what about all the family stories? Stories finding their way down several branches of the family?

We both fell silent just as Bella slipped into the chair next to Carl. "This might be the last chance I'll have to sit until we close," she said.

With hands busy as usual, she filled us in on tonight's entrees. Then Carl and I told her about my discovery of the gold coin. I also summarized my conversations with Chief Sorensen's ancient grandfather.

"I love that story! It's great! It even seems possible. But we'll never really know, will we?" Bella made exclamation points in the air, then twirled both hands in ever lower circles, ending with hands in her lap.

I didn't want to give up on the story. Maybe there was another story, but I believed the real story wouldn't fall to far from the one the Chief's old grandfather had imagined with the help of his long ago girlfriend, Viola. And with only a little help, I'd reached the same conclusions myself.

I made a mental note to talk to Chief Sorensen about his father's stories and see if the Chief thought they were credible. As I brooded silently, Carl brought us back to the present.

"Shouldn't we be talking about the murders? Someone is killing the dog ladies."

And as if on cue, Audrey sailed through the door, a yellow scarf trailing behind her. As she plopped into a chair next to me, she unloosened the scarf and held it out for approval.

"Look at this! Beautiful, right?"

I looked at the lacy scarf knitted with what was probably cotton yarn. I'd knitted a little in my time, but the pattern looked too challenging for me. "It is lovely. Perfect for this time of the year."

Bella pulled it towards her and look it over, eyes squinting at the pattern. She then draped it around her own neck. Audrey grabbed it back and let us know that Chief Sorensen had given it to her.

"And the best part is he knitted himself!"

Chief Sorensen knitted? I remembered the lap blanket draped over the Chief's grandfather's knees and the Afghans over the sofa and chair backs. But how preposterous was that? A police chief who knitted?

"I'll bet he does it only behind closed doors," Carl chimed in.

"Or maybe not." Bella punched Carl on the arm. "Maybe he's just really secure." She stretched out the "really secure" and winked at me.

117

But I wasn't as shocked at the idea of Chief Sorensen as a skilled knitter as I was by the fact that he'd given Audrey the scarf.

"So I guess you helped the Chief a little more. He must have been pleased."

"I talked and talked. He listened and listened," she said as she twirled the yellow scarf about. She sounded happier than I'd heard her in weeks. She also sounded a little tipsy. Did the Chief loosen her up with something more than the gift of a scarf? Or was a romance brewing?

"I told him some more about my troubled nephew and also about my own dysfunctional relationship with my sister. And anything else in my life I thought might be helpful. I told him what I knew about Lydia Harrison...and, oh, more. We talked for a long time about my nephew. "

Bella and Carl knew about Audrey's nephew. They nodded sagely.

"But why would your nephew want to kill Dog Ladies? What motive did he have?" Carl asked. "Something doesn't seem right."

Audrey thought about that for a while as she twisted the scarf through her fingers. "He probably had a motive that made sense to him if not to the rest of the world. I think the Chief will have the answer to all our questions soon. And then we'll all sleep better. That's all I can say."

Either Audrey no longer felt she or any other Dog Lady was in danger, or she was trying to convince us of something she didn't believe herself. Her jovial manner seemed unnatural, bordering on hysteria. Instead of feeling safe, I felt a shiver running up my spine and down my arms.

Audrey slapped a hand down on the table. "Bella, what's for dinner?"

I was more than happy to turn my attention to food.

But I wondered if the danger was over or just beginning. Was it safe to be a Dog Lady?

Chapter 29

The Killer

I've been busy. I'm famous, but I'm not done yet.

She's looking out again, the door opened just a crack to keep any dog inside from slipping out. I remain silent and hidden. The dogs know I'm out here and have been letting her know. I see a row of them at the living room windows, heads bobbing as they bark.

But she can't see me, and in time she'll figure the dogs are hearing a deer or a coyote. I've been watching her for several days, so the dogs are on edge, trying to point her in my direction. By day they crowd into whatever corner of the yard is closest to my hiding spot. Over and over again, they sound the alarm. Ignorant woman. She thinks she is safe. Now the dogs are Inside for the night but not ready to give up their chorus. I see her look in my direction. She moves her head back and forth as if trying to spot whatever the dogs are barking about. She shrugs her shoulders and pulls her head back, closing the door.

Should it be tonight? Or tomorrow afternoon? Afternoons are always fun because they never suspect me. But why not tonight? I'm in a hurry. So many Dog Ladies. So little time. Ha ha. This was all such a brilliant idea and surprisingly fun.

I see her passing in front of the window, calling dogs. Every night she puts them to bed in individual cages lined with cushions. Then she goes to bed herself. Every afternoon at the same time, she takes a bag of treats from a shelf and shakes it, calling "cookie time." And they all run into their cages for their naps, and she heads to the sofa for hers.

I must act at one of those two times when the dogs are all locked away. I hate dogs. And there are too many of them. I shudder to think of 12 dogs knocking me to the ground. Even the tiny ones can be vicious.

I back away from my hiding place, straighten up and brush myself off. This is the right time. I must look my best for this. I follow a footpath back to a dirt road where I've left my car. Inside is the perfect prop. I pull out to the main road and follow it back to her house.

Soon I am knocking on the door. It takes a few minutes before she appears in a white bathrobe. She's looping the tie around her waist as she comes to the door. She peeks through a window at me and I see the tension leave her posture. She opens the door, smiling at what I'm carrying in my arms.

"I'm so sorry to bother you. I thought you might know who owns this little cutie."

Chapter 30

Lois and Barbara are helping me turn the garage into a storage room for filing cabinets that will hold 10 years of files for Redbud Area Dog Rescue. Most of the files now were stashed away in boxes. Audrey has an electronic system for keeping track of her rescue dogs, but she likes to hold on to the paper. Sometimes the original applications contain extra information. For example, just last week, someone called to say she'd found a Yorkshire terrier with one of our microchips. The phone numbers for the woman who'd adopted little Lily were out of service. I researched the name online and found an obituary. Oh oh, I thought. But in the paper file, I found the name and numbers for the woman's daughter. I tried those numbers, but both also were out of service. Finally, I called the vet clinic listed on the application. Bingo. The clinic knew about the dog and provided a working number for the daughter, who was frantic with worry. Lily is now safe at home, and I've updated the microchip information with working phone numbers and Lily's new address.

We frequently help unite lost dogs with their owners, thanks to microchips and tags we send home with every adopted dog. Yesterday I answered a phone call from Mexico, where a dog had escaped from its vacationing owner during a fireworks display. I provided a cellphone and an email and learned the next day that all was well – dog and owner together again.

Lois tugged on her ear as I told the Mexico story. "Those are the things that make us feel so good."

Barbara grunted as she lifted a pile of folders to transfer to the new cabinets in the garage. "How many more boxes do we need to go through?"

I was learning to like these no-nonsense teachers and dog lovers.

"Why do you do this? Fostering homeless dogs and helping Audrey with all the work?" They both looked at me like I was a slow learner. Barbara sat on an overturned cabinet and wiped sweat off her forehead.

"More and more I think life is all about rescuing something. If I'm not rescuing a dog, I'm rescuing an old chair in need of reupholstering. Or I'm trying to rescue a student from a difficult situation on an inappropriate choice," Barbara explained.

"Sometimes she even rescues me from a fashion disaster," Lois said. "She can be very blunt." I laughed. I reserved words like "blunt" for Audrey. Lois and Barbara seemed a little too soft for such a word. I looked at my own dusty and sweaty work clothes, my own fashion disaster, and wondered if my former friends and coworkers would even recognize the new me. For a moment, I wished the pool were still open. Oh for a quick dip in a cool pool.

I suggested we abandon the garage project for the day, and Lois and Barbara agreed with enthusiasm. They much preferred talking about some of their favorite rescue dogs and how those dogs had changed their lives. "Sometimes they rescue us," Lois sighed.

I'd seen the bumper stickers: the ungrammatical "Who Rescued Who?" I knew that many of our foster Parents believed they gained as much or more from helping dogs as the dogs did from their human rescuers.

I'm still not a dog person, but when I'm taking care of the dogs or even helping with the filing system, my feet are solidly on the ground. I feel like I can keep going with my life in spite of all that has happened.

I notice both Lois and Barbara staring at me, waiting for me to say something, I guess.

"You know what? Let's get back to the house. It's been ages since I blogged about one of our dogs. Maybe it's about time. Any suggestions?"

"Write about Fern and Thistle, my two new foster," Barbara said, clapping her hands.

And so I did, as Lois and Barbara sat nearby watching my fingers moving across the keyboard.

We call them the synchronized beagles: Fern and Thistle. If Fern turns left, so does Thistle. If Thistle curls up for a nap, so does Fern. Side by side or following one after the other, they are always together. Should one of them notice that the other has stepped too far away, she will catch up and set things right. They are what we call "bonded." They need to stay together.

I wonder about their history. A rural shelter called us about them. They'd been picked up together as strays and were 8 to 10 years old. No one wanted to adopt them because of their age. After a short transport, they came to safety with us. What sweethearts! Imagine two beagles trying to climb into your lap at the same time. Imagine side-by-side beagle heads resting on their paws at the side of your bed, begging for a lift. Adorable. Someone must have loved them.

But as everyone in the dog rescue world knows, love is not enough when it comes to dog care. We soon learned that both Fern and Thistle had advanced cases of heartworm disease. The vet who saw them said Thistle especially had one of the worst cases she'd ever seen. She could see the worms on the chest x-rays.

Heartworm disease is usually fatal if untreated. The foot-long worms stretch out the arteries and damage the heart and lungs. The disease is preventable if the owner keeps the dog on monthly heartworm pills. Their former owner might have loved Fern and Thistle but also failed to give them the care they needed.

Now we wait. The vet wanted Fern and Thistle on antibiotics and steroids for a month prior to treatment. Then they will receive an injection of an arsenic-based solution that will start killing the worms. The treatment itself can be dangerous if the worms die off too quickly and form clots. That's why caregivers must make sure the dogs stay calm so that their hearts don't overwork.

We're worried about Fern and Thistle, but they're little troopers for sure. In a couple weeks they'll go to the veterinary hospital for their first treatment. A month later, they'll return for more treatment.

At Redbud Area Dog Rescue, we've treated a lot of heartworm dogs, but we've never taken on cases quite this serious. We worry that they may not survive treatment. Sometimes Thistle coughs and wheezes. She has trouble breathing. Fern, although healthier, tires easily.

The future is uncertain for our synchronized beagles. Please keep them in your thoughts.

I showed the blog to Barbara. She wiped a tear from one eye and smiled. In Barbara's language, that's quite a compliment.

Ready to leave, Barbara and Lois stepped outside to say a few words to Audrey, who was trying to show an especially reluctant dog how to walk nicely on a leash. All three (four counting the dog) walked towards the door just as Chief Sorensen's car turned into the driveway.

I watched as he stepped from the car and stood for a moment next to it, sticking his chin forward, his shoulders back. I knew that stance. He was about to bring us bad news.

Chapter 31

Audrey's hands flew to her mouth when she saw Chief Sorensen. She took a seat on the sofa. The rest of us followed suit and pulled up chairs. His face set in granite, the chief told us what we all now suspected.

"I had a call this morning." He cleared his throat and looked at Audrey. "Do you know a Diane Post who runs a dog rescue called Dogs for You Rescue?"

I turned to Audrey, "Isn't that the red-haired lady we saw at the auction?"

Audrey seemed to shrink as she nodded. Somehow I'd expected a shriek or an anguished "Oh no!" But Audrey's voice barely made it above a whisper. "She was one of the good ones. She was a friend." She shook her head as if to shake loose the unpleasant truth. "My nephew? Do they think it was my nephew? He doesn't live more than an hour away from Diane."

The Kansas City police are looking into his whereabouts for the past 48 hours. They also plan to begin 24-hour surveillance based on what I've told them.

"When did it happen?" I asked.

The chief told us that the Missouri officials thought she was killed sometime last night. One of her neighbors found the body this afternoon after becoming suspicious about the nonstop barking. The neighbor found the dogs all in their kennels and Diane on the floor in the dining area. It looked like she'd been sharing a glass of wine with a visitor.

"Another poisoning?" Audrey asked without expecting an answer. "Just like here."

"We'll know more when we have a toxicology report. But yes, it looks very much like poisoning. And nobody anymore believes these deaths are coincidental or suicides. We're all agreed we have a serial killer. A serial killer of women who rescue dogs -- Dog Ladies, if you will."

It I hadn't been so frightened, I might have laughed. Someone was killing Dog Ladies? Why?

As if to answer my question, Chief Sorensen said, "We don't know why. The FBI is now working this case because of all the jurisdictions involved, but the idea of a serial killer targeting Dog Ladies is a new one for everyone. We're not ruling anyone out yet. If we were just looking at one murder, we'd check into people who'd had a bad experience with the rescue group. Maybe they didn't like the dog they adopted. Maybe they didn't receive the refund they expected. Maybe they had some other beef. Some of the more outspoken dog ladies have made enemies with the commercial dog breeders, so we can't rule the breeders out. But would Diane have invited in a breeder for wine and a nice little sit down? Seems unlikely."

As I worked through the possibilities, I kept coming back to the only one that made sense to me.

"Audrey is the link. Audrey may be the real target. The killer can't get to Audrey, so he goes after someone she knows. He sends a message. I'm coming for you, Audrey. I'm getting closer. Be afraid! He's playing with her."

Chief Sorensen smiled at my comments but didn't disagree.

Lois added, "He's scaring more than Audrey. He's scaring all of us. I sure won't open my door to any stranger. And if it's late, I might not even open the door to you, Barbara."

"Same here."

The Chief pointed out, though, that all of the victims had let the killer in to their homes. Even Diane, whose murder came after all the national publicity. She probably would have said the same thing herself last week.

"And she was scared," Audrey added. "When we saw her at the auction, she said as much. She knew someone was killing the Dog Ladies. She told me to be careful, and I told her the same thing."

"And yet she opened her door and invited someone in – at night. Why? Who?" The Chief was asking for thoughts but mainly he seemed to be running the possibilities through his own mind. I wondered if it was time to discard my idea that the murders had something to do with the past, with the ancestors I shared with Audrey and Carl and many others, including Audrey's sister and nephew. Something scratched at my subconscious, but it was an itch I couldn't reach.

The chief grew stern. "The same thing can happen here. I'll be sending patrols past this house frequently, but I expect you all to keep your eyes open and your doors closed. He looked at each of us in turn. Barbara and Lois immediately crossed their hearts. Audrey and I nodded.

"If you see unfamiliar cars, write down a description and a license plate if you can get it. Tell me about unusual calls, emails or other messages."

I thought of the email from Audrey's nephew. Before I could say anything, Audrey told him about the message and agreed to forward it to the Chief's email.

Chief Sorensen started for the door and I followed him. "Is there anything I can do?"

He turned and looked me straight in the eye. "Just stay safe."

"I meant with the investigation, the murders."

"As I said before, just stay safe." Then he added. "But you might come by soon. My grandfather keeps asking about you. He's told me about your conversations." He smiled. "You both share a wild imagination. But the stories gave me a few new ideas about your ancestors."

I didn't quite know what he meant, but I was eager to pay the Sorensen home another visit.

"And will you show me your knitting?"

He stepped outside and firmly closed the door behind him. I turned and looked at three devastated faces looking back at me. We sat together for a while, trying to counsel each other. Lois and Barbara agreed to begin working the phones, telling the other volunteers and foster parents all we knew, warning them to trust no one. We didn't know where the killer might strike next.

Later that evening, Audrey and I turned our thoughts away from the killer of dog ladies to our plans for the weekend's adoption event at a pet supply store in Omaha. I both hoped and feared that Faith the Maltese would find a home and maybe even Scarlet the lab who was no longer the hairless waif she'd been when I first saw her. We needed a

127

good adoption event, not just to place dogs in good home but also to bring money into the dog account. Our vet bills seemed to climb every month, and lately we'd taken in a lot of dogs with expensive veterinary needs, including Fern and Thistle, the beagles with advanced heartworm disease.

Audrey pushed herself out of her chair and stood for a while, bent over enough to rub the knee she said was becoming arthritic. "You know the saying. Growing old is not for sissies."

"You're certainly no sissy," I replied. "I only wish I could face life as bravely as you do."

"Nonsense. You're plenty brave. Braver than you know. I sometimes wish I could be more like you. "

Why she would say such a thing, I didn't know. I don't even want to be me. Audrey continued talking as she walked a little stiffly to the kitchen. "Dog rescue may not pay me a salary, but once in a while, someone drops by with a gift." She returned with a bottle of wine and two glasses. Handing one glass to me, she poured wine to the brim, then filled her own and sat down again.

"I don't recognize the brand, but I tried it last night and soon felt right with the world."

Considering what we knew about the dog lady killings, I wondered if we should be sharing a glass of wine. It seemed somehow dangerous. But I picked up my glass and sipped carefully to draw down the liquid, then placed my glass back on the end table. "Not bad."

Audrey lifted her glass, tilted her head back, and swallowed hard as she drained half of her glass. Not the dainty sipper she. When she placed her glass down, she laughed. "I've never known a wine to act on me so fast. I haven't felt this good since I had laughing gas for a root canal."

At that, I laughed and brought my glass to my lips. I sipped a little deeper and felt a definite tingle. I thought about the night before when Audrey had arrived at Bella's acting a little too happy and slightly tipsy. Had she been sampling this wine then?

We both laughed. Worry seemed so unnecessary. Who cared if someone was killing Dog Ladies? Not us.

One glass of wine left me content and drowsy. I excused myself and danced down the hall to my room. As I turned to wave a few fingers at Audrey, I saw her pour herself another full glass. That night I slept without dreaming. In the morning I woke up Audrey, who'd fallen asleep in her chair.

Should we even be drinking wine with what's going on? Is it safe?

I asked: "Where did this wine come from?"

"A gift from someone who admires my work. That's what it said on the card. Chief Sorensen knows who sent the wine. He dropped the case off earlier this week."

One more reason to visit the chief and his father. I wasn't drinking another drop until I knew more about this gift wine, and I suggested Audrey do the same.

She only yawned, sighed and headed for the shower.

I started getting dogs outside for their first bathroom break of the day and a little exercise. After we'd fed all the dogs and returned emails and phone calls, I had other plans for my day.

Chapter 32

The Nebraska sky chased me to my car as I held an already rain-soaked newspaper over my head. I've never been claustrophobic. I actually like closed-in spaces. They feel safe. But the endless Nebraska sky and the horizons beyond my view -- they scare me. In Missouri the sky was part of a bigger picture that included trees, rocky foothills and other geological structures. In Nebraska the sky is the picture. The trees bend to its wishes. And people like me feel helpless in the sky's grasp.

Once in the car, I backed onto the road and aimed for Chief Sorensen's. We'd stayed busy until after 3 with dog work, so I was afraid the chief's grandfather might be too tired to talk with me. And I was desperate to share some of my concerns with the Chief. Fortunately, I arrived just as Chief Sorensen himself pulled into his driveway. I parked on the street, hurried from my car and rushed to catch up with him.

"I'm worried about Audrey," I said as he turned to face me. "She's always been so strong. Now she doesn't seem like herself. "I started to tell him about waking her up this morning in the chair where she'd fallen asleep after drinking too much wine.

"Slow down. Why are you surprised? Her sister is missing. Someone is killing people she knows, and that person might be her nephew. Don't you think she feels guilty as well as frightened? She built a meaningful life here with her dog rescue group. Now being a Dog Lady is a dangerous thing. And she has to worry about you and everyone else she knows." He rubbed his forehead as if forcing away a pain.

"But I need her to stay the same. I need to lean on her. If she tries to lean on me, I'll topple over. I know I will."

"Judy." He stopped with his hand on the door knob. "I know how much Audrey means to you. I've seen how you've grown stronger. You've changed a lot. You are stronger than you think." And after a pause, he sighed. "And Judy, right now everything can't be about what you need."

He got me there. I couldn't think of a response.

We stepped inside and I saw the old man smiling brightly. I smiled back and stepped close enough to kiss him on the cheek.

"Missed me, didn't you?"

I settled in for a nice chat about my ancestors. To my surprise, Chief Sorensen pulled up a chair and asked if he could listen in,

"So finally my know-it-all son has time to listen to his granddad."

I got things started. "The last time we talked, we ended with Karen arriving in Council Bluffs, Iowa, as a governess. She'd left Denmark suddenly, leaving her children with her brother. We speculated wildly about why she left in a hurry and decided that she might have killed her husband in self-defense and was afraid she'd go to jail – or worse.

The old man nodded. "Left in a hurry, she did. The lovely Viola and I always found that interesting since there are only a few reasons why someone might need to leave the country of her birth in a hurry."

The old man sighed and began to weave a tale about the life of unmarried immigrants in America. Obviously, Karen needed a husband if she was ever going to bring her children over to live with her. That's just the way things were then.

I could imagine the young Karen – then 28 years old and the mother of two, abandoned by her aristocratic lover, beaten by the husband she'd been forced to married, considered by some a murderer, worried that her good looks may already have faded. This young woman now primped her hair, pinched her cheeks, and unfolded the prettiest dress she owned to attend a dance where she might meet eligible bachelors. And what did she find at the dance? Probably no one she thought worthy of her. But as she was preparing to leave, a handsome man dressed in a cowboy hat and boots strolled into the dance. All the girls looked his way. Karen too. But soon she learned he was only a farmer's son, good peasant stock, not for her. She avoided his look. But as is often the case, Johannes wanted the girl who didn't want him.

Chief Sorensen interrupted. "Now that's a true story, for sure. We always want what we can't have."

Johannes wanted the young woman with the wounded air about her, the one who reminded him of a fine lady. He could be worthy of her.

This was America. He was smarter than most of those around him. He'd be a rich man one day. So gradually he won her over.

The old man sighed. "My guess is he told her stories about his adventures in the Old West. That's what I would have done if I'd had any stories to tell. Johannes, he was young and fearless and a gifted story teller to boot. Then once he had her attention, he surprised her with gifts. A necklace. Sapphire earrings. A bolt of silk clothes so she could make herself a new dress."

"Wouldn't she wonder about the money? How could he afford such fine gifts?" I asked.

The old man rubbed his chin and allowed that Karen probably had heard the same stories everyone else had heard about Johannes. According to my own granddad, Johannes was a legend. The lucky Danish gambler who won big and still managed to get home with his skin intact. The young man who made everyone laugh. The ambitious young man who swore he'd be rich someday. If Karen didn't know what everyone else seemed to know, maybe she just decided not to ask too many questions. Here was a man who always seemed to have money. He was buying Nebraska farmland larger than 10 Danish farms. He could sing and play the banjo. And he said he couldn't wait to bring her children to the farm in Nebraska. So what if some would think she was marrying beneath her station. This was America.

So she married him, of course. And within the year, her Danish children arrived -- just in time to greet a baby sister.

"But were they happy?" I wanted them to be happy.

"Here's where I'd like to join the conversation," Chief Sorensen stepped in. He turned first to his grandfather, "And granddad, why haven't you shared these stories with me? Didn't you know I was looking into the Johannes and Karen history?"

"You never asked. I told you I knew everything. You just didn't believe me."

The Chief laughed. "Well now I do." He turned to me.

"I do know about what life was like in the 1870s and 80s when Karen and Johannes settled into life on their Nebraska farm. It wasn't always easy, but here in Eastern Nebraska they were part of a community of settlers, many of them other Scandinavian immigrants. Karen may still have felt she deserved better, but she was the mistress of one of the largest farms in the area. Others envied her for both her position and her handsome husband, who always seemed to have enough extra money to provide good care for his growing family. And here she was free of her past. No one knew of her shame or of the circumstances of her first husband's death. She belonged here with others who were all starting a new life in a new land.

"Ah yes," I said, "but that must have been difficult. She had so many children."

The Chief nodded: "According to one census report, she gave birth to 11 children. But only eight survived past childhood. I found graves for two infants in one of the old cemeteries. Looks like they died shortly after birth. And I found an old newspaper report about the death of one of the children, a 6-year-old girl named Annette. She was the younger of the two children born in Denmark."

I leaned forward to hear the story. One late October day with the temperature dropping, Karen was busy with a new baby while the 9-year-old daughter tended a two-year-old sibling. Always a difficult child, Annette had arrived in America as a 3-year-old with no memory of the mother who had left her behind as an infant. This day she was bored and angry, alternating between tears and temper, and often both combined. Finally Karen suggested Annette "go help your father." And for the rest of the day and into the evening, Karen thought Annette was with Johannes, and Johannes thought Annette was with Karen.

"Oh! I don't want to hear. Don't..." But Chief Sorensen seemed not to understand my distress.

For two days, friends and neighbors searched the fields near the farm house. Finally, someone stumbled over her body nearly covered in leaves. They thought she'd tried to stay warm with a blanket of leaves, but it hadn't been enough.

"Of course, we don't know how well or how poorly they handled the tragedy. I imagine that times were tough for a while. I imagine Karen and Johannes each felt responsible but that they also blamed each other for Annette's death. I can almost imagine their anguish, their arguments.

133

Even the 9 year-old may have felt at least partially responsible. If she'd had time to entertain her sister, things might have been different."

The old man interrupted. "I think they were happy most of the time. That's what Viola thought, and she'd spent some time with them. She said Karen taught her to knit, and Johannes told her stories of his younger years. That's how she knew something about his days as a gambler. What does a child know, of course? But Viola said they seemed to be always near each other, touching, even holding hands at times. "

Chief Sorensen rubbed his hand across his forehead back and forth as he talked. "I've read a lot of diaries and letters from that era. People suffered, they lived difficult lives, but they felt privileged to be part of this great adventure. They saw...they saw..." He hesitated as he searched for the right word. "Poetry? They saw what they were doing, building new lives in a new land, facing so many unknowns, surviving to tell their stories. They saw a kind of poetry, a poetry of the frontier."

We all sat silent for a while. I would not have suspected such sentiment from Chief Sorensen. But then I never would have guessed he enjoyed knitting.

"I'd like to see some of your knitting," I changed the subject.

He smiled. "Later. Right now I think we should – you too, dad – head over to Bella's for dinner.

Between us, we helped the delighted old man out to the car. With his arms across our shoulders and our arms across his back, we were the clothesline to his dangling self. The sky now sparkled as if to apologize for its recent bad temper. When we arrived at Bella's, the Chief carried his father inside and let him pick out a table. He picked the largest table so others could join us. We ordered dinner and drinks while the Chief's grandfather talked and laughed with old friends and new. After I placed a few phone calls, the place filled with more friends and neighbors, most of whom stopped by our table. Audrey came flying through the door with three scarfs twirling about her peasant blouse and a row of bracelets jangling from one arm. Both Lois and Barbara hurried in wearing matching cardigan sweaters. Each sweater displayed grinning dogs carefully knitted along the lower edge. Chief? I looked at the sweaters and back at him. He refused comment and sipped from his soft drink.

134

Lois's college son arrived with his saxophone and played several numbers. A few of the town's teenagers performed numbers from their recent school talent show. But the Chief's grandfather was the true star of the evening, the center of everything. If I live another hundred years, I'll never forget that evening-- the pink in the old man's cheeks, the tears in his eyes, his crackling laughter, and the joy in my heart.

I looked around and knew I was surrounded by friends. Where once I had felt a like an outsider, wondering if everyone was hiding the truth from me, now I knew they were bringing me into their lives in their own cautious ways.

The next morning Chief Sorensen called to tell me his grandfather had died during the night.

Chapter 33

I was on a train sitting next to a man I didn't recognize. My sister was with us. She got up to find something to eat or to use the bathroom and didn't return. After a while I started looking for her. I walked from one car to another, all of them packed with people, many of whom were standing in the aisles. I couldn't find her and just as I woke up I remembered I didn't have a sister.

Will these dreams never stop? Always about losing things. And losing people. Can I just tell my subconscious to quit bothering me? I get the message. Stop.

Yet here again, I'm losing someone – an ancient man I'd known for such a short time but who had become important in my life. When I heard of his death, I was still warm from the evening's gaiety. That bubbly feeling that had been so long absent from my life now refused to leave. For two days I couldn't stop smiling. And when I thought of my old friend's death, I saw only the way he looked that last night at Bella's. The story of Annette's death should have saddened me, and at the moment it did. I'd sniffed back tears and tried not think of how much the story matched my own. But like Johannes and Karen, I survived and by God I loved the evening that followed. I wouldn't have missed it for anything.

The local newspaper made a big deal about the death of Lars Sorensen. He was the oldest man in the county. In the days before the funeral, I worked hard to prepare for an upcoming dog adoption event, and I nearly forget about the killer stalking Dog Ladies. Audrey kept busy too, but I'm pretty sure the Dog Lady killer was the first thing in her mind every morning and her last thought every night. She'd been her usual Audrey self at Bella's, but I knew she was faking some of her good humor. At home, she seemed elsewhere, seldom speaking. I'd see her standing by a window, waiting it seemed for something or someone. In the evening, she'd pour herself a glass of the wine we'd shared a few nights ago. And each time she drank some of the gift wine, she fell asleep in her chair. I'd forgotten to ask Chief Sorensen who'd given Audrey the wine. I could wait on that until after the funeral. Meanwhile, I avoided drinking the wine myself and put the bottle away before Audrey could drink too much. That was pretty easy since even one large goblet full was enough to make her drowsy. I'd try to get her to bed, but she always insisted she wanted to sit and think a bit more.

Audrey had plenty to think about. We now had six murdered Dog Ladies. The killer had been quiet since the death of Diane in Missouri. Audrey's sister was still missing, as was her nephew who was still the prime suspect. We were learning more about Lydia Harrison every day. I'd met her daughter when she arrived in Redbud to collect her mother's belongings and arrange for her burial. We'd exchanged numbers and emails.

The day of the adoption event we loaded eight dogs into the van, including my little Faith and the Blue Lady, the Sheltie from the auction. Several foster parents would meet us at the pet supply store with their own foster dogs. I knew by the small crowd waiting just inside the door that we were going to have a good day. Several people helped us unload crates, dogs, and a table for all our supplies. Soon we were ready to begin. Coco and Scarlet hated being in cages and began barking incessantly, so I asked a couple of our teenaged volunteers to please give the two noisy dogs enough attention to quiet them down. Then I explained to some of the onlookers that Coco and Scarlet "are really quiet dogs at home." I'm not sure they believed me.

I turned and almost bumped into a middle-aged woman with a Maltese walking beside her on a leash. The little dog sported a pink harness and a sequined collar. "We've come to meet Faith," the lady said. With half cheer and half fear, I pulled Faith from her cage and suggested we go find a peaceful corner. Once away from the noise (Scarlet and Coco were still barking), I placed Faith on the floor next to the lady's dog. Faith took a step closer to the other dog and then another step until the two little white dogs seemed nearly glued to one another. Faith had come so far since the day I'd walked her away from Old Man Schmidt's puppy mill, but I knew she still needed more socializing. She would do well with a companion dog that could show her how to be a pet. Faith liked what she saw and the lady with her little dog just nodded and smiled. "How do I go about taking home this little darling?"

While I began talking to the lady about Faith and our adoption contract, I noticed several people already filling out applications for some of our other dogs. Audrey seemed busy talking to someone about Sprout, a young chocolate lab mix. Lois whispered, "Three people want Blue Lady!"

Three hours later, I looked at a row of mainly empty cages. Some dogs were now officially in new homes. Volunteers were driving a few others to "home visits" with potential adopters. Coco and Scarlet had stopped barking but hadn't yet attracted adopters.

"All in all, a good adoption day," Audrey said to all of us as we gathered to hear her report. "If all these adoptions go through, we'll have placed 10 dogs today."

"Yahoo!" Lois shouted. Several others joined in. I love these victories. We'd adopted out dogs that had run out of all their second chances only to find rescue at the last minute. Some of them were going home with people so wonderful I wish they'd adopted me. Everyone seemed satisfied with the new homes although a couple potential placements were still contingent on satisfactory call backs from references.

"And this means we can take in a few new dogs," Audrey said. Golden words.

Before today I'd told everyone who called that we were out of space, no room for any new dogs. Next week we could say "yes" to a few dogs in need. I might just volunteer to visit a few county shelters next week and pluck a few dogs off death row.

As we loaded crates and supplies into the van, I scratched a sad-eyed Coco behind the ears. "Your day will come. Maybe I'll write a blog about you. Maybe I'll title it "What's Wrong with Coco?"

By the time we turned into the driveway at home, I was ready to write.

What's wrong with Coco?

Coco is a 2 to 3 year old dog who is perfect in most of the important ways. She's housebroken, cuddly, friendly, good with children and other pets, and a nice size to boot – only about 35 lbs. She's not too old or too young. Not too small. Not too big. Just right.

At night when I'm watching television, she tucks herself against me. She also joins me in bed, burrowing under the covers, sometimes dropping her head lightly over my waist.

Am I the only one who thinks she's a wonderful dog?

I picked up Coco from one of our nearby shelters where she'd been picked up as a stray. She was infested with fleas. Her frantic scratching had worn away much of her hair. No owner claimed her, and I doubt the shelter officials would have released her to an owner who had neglected her so badly.

We took her in, got rid of the fleas, and restored her coat to something almost luxurious. But still she waits for someone to come along and offer her a home.

Why? I asked one of our other volunteers. The answer shocked me.

"She's not the most attractive dog," the other person said.

"I think she is," I answered.

"But you're used to her."

Oh? I looked at Coco closely. I guess you'd call her a plain black and tan dog. "But she has such a pretty face," I respond.

"If you say so."

Discussing her prospects, we decided Coco might attract more attention with a bright collar and maybe a scarf.

So watch for Coco at our next adoption event sporting a bright collar and a festive scarf.

And tell her she's beautiful.

I posted my blog just as Audrey finished filing away the paperwork on today's adoptions. She'd also entered the adoption fees and adopters' information on the appropriate databases.

"Time to feed the dogs," Audrey said.

Chapter 34

I'm in a meeting with six people; we're talking about a missing camera. A lost camera. Does anyone remember seeing it? They all turn to look at me. They think I'm responsible. They think I lost the camera. No, worse. They think I stole the camera. They don't say it, but I know they are thinking it. Then something happens and I'm supposed to join two other people, but they hurry away from me as quickly as possible. They don't want me with them. I can't catch up. I follow but end up lost in a many-storied building. I take the elevator up and down, up and down, trying to find the way out. I'm about to ask for help when an alarm rings out.

The phone. The phone. Why doesn't Audrey answer the phone! I pull a pillow over my head.

I usually wake to the sounds of Audrey in the kitchen. This morning I wake to the phone sounding like an alarm. Judy! Judy! Finally the phone stops. I pull away the pillow and listen for the morning sounds of Audrey clattering about in the kitchen and whistling softly. That's how I know it's time to wake up. No Audrey sounds. Nothing. I close my eyes and pull the blanket up to my chin. I can sleep a little longer.

The phone. The phone. Is she sleeping in for a change? The phone calls me like an alarm. Judy! Judy! I throw off the blanket and stomp into the bathroom. I squint into the mirror and see a creased face with blue circles under the eyes. I see my hair blossoming in wild tufts and waves. Oh, Judy. Maybe you should try a little harder with your appearance. Deciding that Audrey is sleeping in, I pull on my new jeans and t-shirt and begin letting dogs outside. I start my coffee and walk into the living room where I see Audrey asleep in her chair, a near-empty wine glass on the table next to her.

"Audrey." I say her name softly and nudge her shoulder. No response. "Audrey!" I speak louder and punch her shoulder. No response. "AUDREY! AUDREY! I grab both of her shoulders and shake vigorously while continuing to shout her name. Her head flops back and forth. I feel for a pulse. She has one...a faint one. I drop her back in the chair and dash for the phone.

After what seems like an hour but is actually only a few minutes, an ambulance squeals up the driveway and two paramedics race for the door, both swinging bags of medical equipment at their sides. I hold open the door and point them towards Audrey, explaining as they kneel down by her just how I'd found her. I chatter about the wine, the gift wine and its alarming properties. The female medic sniffs at the wine glass and asks me to find any more of the same wine.

I'm twisting my hands and asking questions. "Is she going to be ok?" The male medic (are they always in male/female pairs?) waves a hand my way as if to say "Leave us alone. Be still." He's bending over Audrey with one hand on her neck. He nods at his partner who produces an oxygen max which she slips over Audrey's nose and mouth. Then together they lift her onto the stretcher and move towards the door.

The dogs are all outdoors, many of them crowded at the door. I look out to make sure no one is causing trouble.

One of the medics looks back at me as they carry Audrey out the door. He tells me which hospital they're taking her to.

"Find someone who will drive you there. And drive slowly."

I find my phone and call Chief Sorensen.

"Slow down," he keeps saying. "I can't understand what you're saying."

I take a deep breath. "It's Audrey!" I shout into the phone. "She's in an ambulance on the way to Immanuel Hospital. I found her unconscious this morning. I think that wine you brought her made her sick."

"What wine?"

The ambulance pulls out of the driveway and takes off with siren blaring. Startled, I drop the phone and it slides across the floor. I can hear Chief Sorensen repeated the question, "What wine?"

"What wine?" he asked again as I returned my phone to my ear. I told him about the wine Audrey had been drinking. "She said you dropped it off and that it was a donation from someone. "She's fallen asleep in her chair every night she's had some of that wine"

141

And then oh my God I realized this was all my fault.

"I meant to tell you about it the last day with your father. We took off for Bella's and I completely forgot. I knew there was something different about that wine. It was just too good to be true. A few sips and I was giddy silly."

His response was slow and mournful. "I found the box of wine on her doorstep and brought it in. I don't know who sent it. I thought she knew who sent it. Oh my God." I could almost see him dropping his head into his hands.

I knew we were both thinking about the killer of Dog Ladies. Had he found a way around Audrey's defenses?

By why, I wondered, hadn't Audrey been more suspicious. Why hadn't I? We both knew there was something different about that wine, different enough that I decided to leave it alone. Why didn't I say something to Audrey about my concerns?

How could we all be so stupid when we knew we should be so careful?

I sighed into the phone – a short burst of air.

The Chief said he'd be right over and he'd drive me to the hospital. I started feeding dogs and then called Barbara to see if she and Lois could come over and finish feeding and exercising the dogs. After shouting a startled "NO!" when she heard what had happened, she rallied and said she'd be right over. I also knew these two ladies would let the rest of our group know what had happened. By the time Audrey woke up, her room would be floating in flowers and balloons.

If she woke up.

I poured some of the wine into a Mason jar and capped it just in time to hand it over to Chief Sorensen as he arrived to drive me to the hospital.

"I'll drop this off at the county lab but I'm pretty sure what we'll find. Someone mixed a barbiturate in with the wine. My guess is phenobarbital. That's been the culprit in all of these dog lady murders."

I knew that phenobarbital was used as a sleep aide and also to treat seizure disorders in humans as well as dogs. We had a couple dogs taking phenobarbital. We talked about the suicides of several well-known

142

persons who'd taken overdoses of phenobarbital. And we remembered again about the cult that had committed mass suicide by drinking orange juice laced with a lethal about of phenobarbital.

Had Audrey ingested a lethal amount? I clutched my purse and started twisting it in my hands.

As if reading my mind, Chief Sorensen said, "This wasn't like the other cases where one glass contained a killer amount of phenobarbital. But it sounds like she drank enough for a serious overdose."

With that he turned on the light and siren.

We charged into the hospital ER and rushed to the nurses' station. I blurted out Audrey's name and asked where we could find her. A young nurse with a ridiculously perky nose took her time responding after first checking out my uncombed hair and lack of makeup. "They're working on her now." She pointed to the rows of chairs in the waiting area. "Take a seat."

The Chief flashed his badge and said he needed to talk to the doctor in charge. "This is a police case." Thank you, Chief Sorensen. The nurse stepped away from the counter and disappeared behind a curtain. A minute or so later she returned with a woman in a white coat, apparently the doctor in charge. The nurse pointed at us.

"I'll take care of this. You find us a couple coffees."

He stepped away from me and towards the doctor. I watched as they talked, both heads bowed and almost touching, the doctor with her hands clutched behind her back. Both nodded as they talked. Then something the Chief said startled the doctor or maybe someone called for her. Her head snapped up and she spun towards the curtain behind her. With two long strides she disappeared behind the curtain. I could hear excited voices. Oh my God. What's happening? A couple more white-coated men rushed past the curtain. The Chief tried to follow but found a burly attendant blocking his way. He stood where he'd stopped, arms now dangling. He waited. I waited. Oh Audrey. Oh Audrey. What's going on? Shouting! What's all the shouting about?

A couple minutes later the doctor stepped back out and talked to Chief Sorensen again. I saw her blowing air out of puffed up cheeks and then shaking her head slowly. She moved her hands about nervously as she talked. Oh No! No way was I running for coffee! Is Audrey alive? I wanted to shout. Seeming to hear my distress, the Chief turned around and motioned me towards him.

"She's alive," he told me quietly. "But she's a long way from out of the woods." The doctor excused herself and walked away.

"Her heart stopped, but they were able to bring her back. They've also had to intubate to help her breathe. They're taking other steps to get the phenobarbital out of her system, but they can't promise she'll make it. "

I covered my mouth and nose with both hands. I closed my eyes. I don't like to cry. I'm not sure I have any tears left in me. I don't believe in prayer. I didn't know what to do.

The chief touched my shoulder. "They're taking her to the Intensive Care Unit. The next 24 hours are critical."

I can't speak. I can't take my hands away from my face.

"If you hadn't been there this morning, she would have died. You probably saved her life."

"If she lives," I reminded him, speaking through my hands. "If she lives. If I'd stayed up later or gotten up earlier, that would have made a difference. I should have hid the wine. I should have thrown it away. If she dies, I'll blame myself. It will be my fault. Again, something terrible will be my fault. And I forgot to ask you about the wine. If I'd remembered, we wouldn't be here now wondering if she will live or die."

He looked at me with an expression of what? Pity? Compassion? Disgust? I don't know.

"And if I'd been a little suspicious about the wine, if I'd made sure Audrey knew where it came from, if if if. This is not your fault, Judy. Someone tried to kill her – and might have killed you too – with this tainted wine. That person is to blame, not you."

We looked for signs to the ICU and found a coffee machine along the way. Before we found the ICU waiting room, the Chief spoke as if to no one or any one, as if he were talking to himself.

"And sometimes terrible things happen and no one is to blame."

I looked at him. I knew what he was trying to say.

I couldn't respond.

And so the waiting began. We sat. We paced. We sat. I began calling the others. After an hour, the room started to fill with Audrey's volunteers. Even a few people from other rescue groups appeared, all rooting for Audrey's recovery. Some prayed. Some talked. Some pressed fingers to their heads as if they were mentally sending Audrey messages. Live, Audrey. Fight, Audrey.

Carl and Bella closed the restaurant and came quietly into the waiting room, still wearing matching khakis and yellow tunics. Bella was so frightened she couldn't move her hands, and without her hands she had trouble talking. Carl led her to a chair and sat in one next to her, his mustache seeming longer and sadder than ever.

Lois and Barbara arrived looking as if they'd been running. They charged in and stopped so suddenly I thought they'd fall over. They looked around the room until they found me and sat down on either side of me, each of them holding on to one of my arms. Chief Sorensen, who'd been pacing, leaned towards us and said he needed to leave.

"Things are happening. I've heard from Kansas City and from the FBI. I can't tell you any more now, but I do need to run. I also need to drop off a sample of the tainted wine with the FBI lab. We know what it is, but some testing might tell us more."

He looked from Lois to Barbara. "Can you get Judy home?" And he almost saluted as he turned to stride out of the room.

And so we waited. An hour passed. Then two. Some of the volunteers left for home, promising to be back later. Another hour. Another. I paced. Five hours. Six hours. Seven hours. Everyone is so kind to me. I don't understand why. Audrey is as important to them as she is to me.

Eight hours. Nine hours. Someone comes in with fried chicken and coleslaw. We nibble around the edges. We wait. We pace. Every once in a while a nurse or doctor steps into the room and we surround the poor person.

"No change." The response is always the same. "No change."

Barbara suggests she take me home for a couple hours. We drive back to Audrey's place, ready to feed and exercise the dogs. We race through the feedings. I throw balls too vigorously. I run with some of the younger dogs. I cuddle one little dog after another. I see Barbara doing the same, and finally she says, "Enough? Can we go back to the hospital now?" We put the dogs back in their kennels. Some protest. You think a dog can't pout?

Ten hours. Eleven hours. We wait. "No change."

At 2 a.m., a doctor steps into the waiting room and smiles. He puts up one hand as if to keep us away from him. He nods. "She's awake. She's going to be ok."

We cheer. Lois hugs the doctor, who wiggles out of her grasp, nodding and backing away. "You should all go home now," he said. "She won't be ready for visitors until sometime tomorrow. If all goes well, she'll be home in a couple days."

Chapter 35

I heard the laughter from down the hall and recognized Audrey's voice. Stepping into the room, I knew I was in the right place for 20 other reasons – the number of balloon and flower arrangements positioned around the room.

Sitting next to Audrey with her hands on the bed rail was a slim, long-haired woman I knew much be Audrey's daughter. I'd called her during our waiting room occupancy and knew she was flying in from San Francisco. Now both Audrey and her daughter seemed convulsed by laughter so intense it had both of them in tears.

Audrey gulped back a few laughter hoots and waved me towards her. Judy, meet my daughter Sarah. As if I haven't already been through enough, she's now trying to kill me with laughter.

Sarah stood and reached across the bed to shake my hand. She looked at me with clear green eyes and a wide mouth that smiled easily. Her dark hair hung straight to her shoulders. In her other hand, she dabbed at a tear running down her cheek.

"All I did," she started to explain but broke into laughter again. She swiped at her tears again. "All I did was remind her of when I was 12 years old." They both exploded as if that line alone was the funniest quip any comedian ever delivered.

"Let me tell it." Audrey sat up straighter in her bed.

"She's 12, right? She can't drive, so she has to depend on her mother to drive her places. But she's also at that age when she finds it embarrassing that she even has a mother."

"Oh mom, please, I wasn't that bad."

"But you did find me embarrassing that day. Audrey turned my way and continued. "So I'm driving, and she and two friends are chattering away in the back seat. The radio is playing her favorite station –not, I might add, NPR. A song came on that I actually liked, so I started singing along."

They both burst into new peals of laughter.

Sarah interrupted, "But MAAAAHM." She was obviously channeling her 12-year-old self.

"Let me tell it," Audrey takes us both in. "So all of a sudden I notice this stone silence coming from the back seat. Then out of the silence emerges the humiliated voice of my young daughter saying, "But MAAAHM. That's OUR music."

They both threw back their heads and laughed again.

"What could I say?" To this day I don't remember how I answered, or if I did. I probably just kept my mouth shut. After that, I could never take her anywhere without her first reminding me not to sing."

Audrey looked at her daughter. "Ah, it's so good to have you here."

Sarah patted her mother's arm. "It's good for me to see you at all. I just can't believe someone would try to kill you. All this business about someone killing dog ladies. It just doesn't make sense."

"Now you need to tell me about my two grandchildren. I wish they'd come along."

"I figured it was best the boys stayed home with their father. When I was racing to the airport, I wasn't sure what I'd find when I got here. You were still very critical."

Sarah then turned to me. "I understand we should all be thanking you. You're the one who got her to the hospital in time."

I wasn't sure I deserved the thanks, but I accepted it. I stammered something about wishing I could have done more and being so happy she was alive and could still laugh until she cried. Everyone should be so blessed.

Just in time two other dog foster parents poked their heads in the room, saving me from embarrassing myself further.

Audrey greeted the newcomers and went through the introductions again. She kept the mood light but just for a moment I saw her expression change, as if she'd seen something that frightened her. She knew and I knew that we could not relax. Someone was still killing dog ladies and that someone still wanted to kill Audrey.

Audrey's room filled with a couple more visitors who rushed to Audrey's bedside. They seemed too overcome to speak. Then a few more arrived and a few more after that. With all the visitors, balloons and flowers packed together and everyone talking at once, we attracted the attention of a nurse who poked her head through the door and frowned. She pronounced Audrey tired although Audrey seemed anything but tired. The nurse persisted. "I'm sure she appreciates visitors, but we'd like to send her home in a day or two. That won't happen if we don't give her time to rest and recover."

Grumbling, we filed out of the room, waving and blowing kisses as we left. Sarah stayed behind at her mother's bedside. As I stepped out the door, I suddenly remembered a few messages I needed to pass on and stepped back in. "The Get Well wishes are pouring in. Facebook is all about you today, Audrey. Most of the emails too. For a change, we don't have that many calls or emails from people wanting to give up their dogs."

I pulled a folded piece of paper out of my purse and started reading out names and messages. Audrey nodded at each time, smiled at most, and frowned at one or two. "Sylvia wishes me well? I thought she hated me."

"Oh, mother."

"Don't you mean..." They both threw back their heads and howled in unison. "But MAAAHM!"

The same nurse stepped in the room and cleared her throat. We didn't need to hear her speak.

A few minutes later Sarah and I were on the elevator discussing living arrangements at Audrey's. Sarah had a suitcase with her since she'd come directly from the airport to the hospital.

"I hope you don't mind sleeping with dogs."

Sarah laughed. "I look forward to it."

"I also hope you don't mind if we make a quick stop on the way home. I need to buy something appropriate to wear to the funeral of a 110-year-old man."

Whatever I found, I hoped I wouldn't need it again for a long time.

Chapter 36

The Killer

I'll need a new plan for Audrey. To me honest, I wasn't sure I even wanted to use the same method for her. The other Dog Ladies weren't important. I was willing to kill them kindly. You might say I did them all a favor letting them just sleep away their miserable lives.

They didn't know me. I didn't know them. It was easy. But it's different when you know the person and that person knows you.

It was a crazy idea thinking I could just leave some tainted wine on her doorstep and she might drink enough to die fast. But I just wasn't ready to kill her face to face.

Now I think I am.

I've been reading all the chatter online. I'm actually one of her Facebook friends although I'm sure she doesn't know that. She sees my name – the name I use on Facebook – and thinks I'm just another rescue person.

I learned of her near death and miraculous (tired of that word) survival on Facebook. Everyone is posting comments. Everyone is sharing. Blah. By now Audrey might even have made the television news. I was disappointed to hear of her survival, of course, but now I'm thinking this was all for the best.

She's got to be scared. She's bound to be careful. Others will be watching out for her too.

I must decide what to do next. I need to be careful. I like the recognition, but I really don't want to get caught.

What next? Another warning?

Or straight to Audrey?

Face to face with Audrey?

Chapter 37

Half the town of Redbud turned up for Lars Sorensen's funeral. At least it seemed that way to me. The church choir sang "Amazing Grace" and Lois's son played a mournful saxophone solo that brought tears even to the eyes of somber Scandinavians.

Several Redbud residents stepped up to say a few things about the ancient man. One elderly man laughed and cried through a short eulogy that included references to chasing frogs, kissing girls, skinny dipping, and meeting in their secret clubhouse. I wondered if he could really have been a contemporary of Chief Sorensen's grandfather. He looked to be late 80s or even 90s but that still would not have put him in the same generation. Maybe he was calling on his own childhood memories. Finally a woman stepped up to the old man, thanked him, and led him back to a spot in the first pew.

Chief Sorensen told about meeting his grandfather for the first time.

"I was 7 years old, a bewildered kid who'd just lost both his parents in an automobile accident. And here I was being dropped off at the home of a grandparent I'd never met before. He probably hadn't been around a young boy in about 40 years. My first impression? He scared the living daylights out of me!"

The Chief looked up and smiled at the laughter his remarks evoked.

"If you knew him at all, you knew he could stop any boy in his tracks with just one look." The Chief stopped and narrowed his eyes in an imitation of his grandfather's look. "I find that particular look useful in my current profession." A few more listeners laughed or nodded as if remembering the Lars Sorensen look.

"After a week with my granddad, I knew he was really an old softie. We had our problems now and then over the years. He was already an old man when he took me in. He had to learn how to take care of a young boy, and I had to learn, well, I just had a lot to learn. He never let me forget that.

"He took me fishing. He helped me with my homework. He taught me several card games and made sure I knew how to win. And I do know how to win. " He paused and waited for the laughter to die out again.

"I think there were a lot of people in town then who wondered if Lars Sorensen had any business trying to raise a young boy. Well, he showed them all. I couldn't have asked for a better parent."

I wanted to applaud.

Later, after the service at the cemetery, I told Chief Sorensen how much I enjoyed his remarks and also I much I liked his grandfather.

He thanked me and walked with me to my car.

"How is Audrey?"

"Coming home tomorrow. She seems to have made a complete recovery. She's happy about having her daughter here for a visit."

"Oh that's good.

He walked with his hands linked behind his back.

"I just wish I we could catch the person who's doing this. Some of it still doesn't make sense to me."

I waited for him to go on.

"We're looking at a mass murderer here, but one who uses a method that might lead authorities to suspect suicide instead of murder. Why? And phenobarbital is a rather gentle way of killing someone. Again, that doesn't sound like our typical mass murderer. With mass murderers, we think more of guns, knives, torture. At least that's the way it is with male murderers."

"Females?"

"Females are more likely to use poison."

"Oh!" Was he suggesting that a woman was killing the Dog Ladies? And that a woman was targeting Audrey? I immediately thought of Audrey's sister, Jessica. She was still missing. It was as if she'd come out of hiding for a few days and then disappeared again. But I think we all feared that her son may have killed her, the son who seemed a more likely candidate for mass murder than his mother. And hadn't Jessica been afraid of her son? Hadn't he been the reason she chose to walk away after 911?

The Chief pointed out some of the things Audrey had said about her relationship with her sister. "We'd be foolish to not at least consider Jessica a person of interest," he said.

"I still see the nephew as the logical suspect? He's the one with the history. He might have killed someone when he was 14. His wife died of phenobarbital poisoning. He's been seen around here. He even came to Audrey's place once saying he was looking for his mother. And I'm sure some men use poison to kill."

The Chief then ticked off a few other concerns. "It's odd that the only place we found fingerprints was at the site of Lydia Harrison's murder. We have only the killer's own statements to connect all these murders. "

"And it seems odd that the killer claimed responsibility for all the murders. At least it seems odd to me. At first the killer was fine with not attracting attention. Then the killer claimed responsibility for all the murders by sending letters to television stations. "At first it was hush hush. Then Hello World. Look at me. Look what I'm doing."

Chief Sorensen thought about that and then raised a hand as if to stop me. "To me, that's not so odd. Maybe the killer thought someone would make the connection earlier. A lot of serial killers want the recognition. They enjoy playing games with the investigators and believe they are smarter than those trying to catch them.

The Chief then agreed that the nephew may be the logical suspect, but he added, "The Kansas City authorities say he's lived a quiet, even respectable life there. His coworkers are surprised by his absence since he's been one of those who never calls in sick. They all describe him as gentle and law abiding. Odd to say the least. And I have to wonder why he would be obsessed with Audrey. Wouldn't his more likely target be his mother? Audrey's sister, Jessica?"

"Yes. And he may already have killed her."

"Then why didn't that end the murders? And why kill the other Dog Ladies? I still can't figure out why the killer would target Dog Ladies. That seemed like a road to Audrey, not to his mother."

I wondered. Did Audrey do something to outrage her nephew? Something we didn't know about? Something maybe even she didn't know about?

I also knew the words "Dog Lady" weren't always a compliment. I thought of Dog Ladies as women like Audrey who ran reputable dog rescue organizations, rescuing dogs, giving them good care, and finding them new homes. But other people thought of Dog Ladies as hoarders, crazy women who collected dogs and often kept dozens with them in conditions unfit for dogs or humans.

I asked Chief Sorensen if any of the known victims fit into the category of hoarders. "Do we have any idea who the first victim might have been?"

"We may never know that. We're looking closely at the first known victim, but there could have been earlier ones."

I stepped into my car and closed the door. Rolling down the window, I called after Chief Sorensen as he walked away.

"I'll be picking up Audrey in the morning. She'd love it if you stopped by. We'd all feel safer."

He touched his forehead in a quick salute and moved on after leaving me with one more comment. "And please call me Randy."

I had trouble calling him anything but Chief Sorensen. Only Audrey seemed comfortable calling him Randy to his face.

As he left, I wondered if it seemed strange returning to an empty house.

Chapter 38

I'm driving home but I'm not sure to which home. I'm on my usual route. I'm sure of that. But the road ends. I know of another route home, so I back up, turn around and head to the other road. I'm nearly home when a police car stops me. The officer steps out and asks, "Why do you always take that other road? It's the wrong one."

This dream confuses me. Am I taking the wrong road in my life? If so, I'm not sure where I'll find the right road. Or is my dream telling me something about the killer of the dog ladies? Are we all on the wrong path to catching the killer?

I push aside several dogs, and step out of bed. It's up to me to take care of all the morning chores, so I don't waste any time getting started. I think I hear Sarah moving about in her room. "Come on critters." I yawn and yawn again as I begin the process of feeding them and releasing them outside. Why am I so tired? I rest my head on the kitchen counter as I wait for my first cup of coffee. I turn my head to one side when I hear Sarah's voice.

"Just point me in the right direction. I'm here to help."

Working together, we feed all the dogs – upstairs and downstairs—and spend some time with all of them outdoors. Scarlett, Coco and a couple new dogs circle the yard like dogs in a race. As they came hurtling in our direction, both Sarah and I flattened ourselves against the side of the house. Whew! "You know I'm not really a dog person," I said, and she laughed and added, "And you know I never had a dog growing up."

"What?!" That didn't seem possible. I couldn't even imagine Audrey as someone living without at least one dog. Then Wiley, a leggy White German Shepherd mix skidded to a stop in front of me and placed two muddy paws on my shoulders. The other new dog, Nala the Husky mix, stopped running long enough to roll in a puddle. Oh no! When will I have time to bathe dogs? Then I thought, wished, that maybe the mud would dry and just drop off or blow away. I sighed.

"You didn't have a dog growing up?" It was starting to sound reasonable. We're were watching nine dogs playing in the yard around out. Another nine small dogs trotted about in the small yard off the walk-out basement. We needed to spend at least a little time supervising the little dogs before returning them inside.

"No. Oddly, Audrey got her first dog when I went away at to college."

I looked at her. "And the rest, as they say, is history."

"She let me name that dog. He became Leon, a brown Dobie/Collie mix. And she really loved that dog. Once or twice I even heard her talking baby talk to him. I don't think she even did that with me.

Audrey spoke baby talk to a dog? Impossible, I thought. She would never do that if she thought anyone was listening. She left that kind of behavior to Lois and Barbara and those of their sentimental ilk.

"I heard it. I really did." Sarah turned her back just as Coco leaped up towards her. Then she went down on her knees and turned to embrace the excited dog at ground level. "Then a few years after adopting Leon, she became involved with a rescue group in California and ended up keeping an incorrigible American Eskimo who'd been returned three times as being "hopeless."

"And a few years after that, she moved here. She'd been interested in her ancestors here and decided she'd like to live somewhere people didn't talk about their "life style" but rather just their "life.""

That sounded like Audrey.

"I'm not sure she'd thought about starting her own dog rescue group here, but she did so not too long after settling in. And look what's she's done. I'm so proud of her." Sarah pulled her hair out of the clasp holding it back, shook her head vigorously, and pulled in back again smoothly, snapping the clasp back in place. "And by the way, I remember a time when mom said she wasn't a dog person either." She looked at me and grinned like a Cheshire Cat.

I'm ready when you are," she said.

"Just a few more things we need to do first." We returned the big dogs to their crates and went down to play awhile with the little dogs.

156

Mopping, dish washing and other tasks would wait until we returned from picking up Audrey.

"Did Audrey ever tell you what she found out about her ancestors?" I figured Audrey had already told her I was a distant cousin.

"She said she learned a lot, but I'm not sure what she meant by that. And you're not the only distant relative she's met while researching her family."

I knew that too, thinking of Carl, but Audrey may not have mentioned everything she learned or everyone she met. I remembered that Carl and Bella had talked about how hard Audrey had laughed when she found out they were in Nebraska to research her ancestors who were also Carl's ancestors.

After spending time with the little dogs, I checked emails and answered a few calls. One email, the most interesting one, would wait until we were back from the hospital. It was from Lydia Harrison's daughter and it included an attachment titled "diary." This could be important. But I dared not open it yet because I knew it might lead to a long delay. Audrey was probably already wondering where we were.

Twenty minutes later we arrived at the hospital and found Audrey in her room talking with Lois and Barbara. We'd brought Audrey the change of clothes she'd requested – Jeans and a long purple tunic. While she changed, we waited outside her room. Then we all took turns wheeling her to the hospital exit. . She scowled at the hospital policy that kept her in a wheel chair until she stepped outside.

"Ridiculous. I ought to fall over now just for effect."

But she didn't fall over, and within minutes we were on our way back home.

As we pulled in the driveway, we saw Chief Sorensen sitting on the front step.

"Hey Randy," Audrey called.

Although I'd asked him to stop by, we all approached the house with the fear that he might be bringing more bad news. As if noticing our concern, he quickly put up both hands as if to stay "stop."

"No bad news." He looked at Audrey. "I just wanted to welcome you home."

157

"And except for your recovery, there's no good news either."

We all stepped inside and he updated us on the investigation. In spite of hard work by detectives in several states, we had not learned anything new. A few false leads had led nowhere. But Audrey's sister and her nephew seemed to have disappeared without a trace.

If Jessica was still alive, she already knew how to disappear and stay disappeared if that was what she wanted. But what about her son? What about Charles? Wherever they were, were they together? Were they both still alive?

As we were mulling some of this over among ourselves, the phone interrupted us.

Audrey stood up to grab the phone. Soon we were all out the door.

Chapter 39

The call was from the man who'd adopted Blue Lady, the Sheltie from the auction. Blue had bolted out their front door and was running loose in the neighborhood. They'd tried to catch her, but Blue was in a panic and running from anyone who came close to her – including her new family. Audrey handed the phone to me so I could take down directions while she found stouter walking boots.

"We don't know what to do. We're afraid she'll run onto a busy street," Ira said, in a voice that told me he might have just come back from chasing Blue Lady. He stopped to catch his breath. "She was doing so well, sleeping on our bed, going on walks. She was still scared, but she was starting to accept us. Now she won't come to us when we call her."

"We'll be right there," I assured him. "Audrey has a lot of experience catching scared dogs, and Blue Lady probably knows me better than anyone." I'd just finished writing down his directions when Audrey grabbed back the phone.

"Start making up some fliers we can pass out to your neighbors. We'll be there in about 20 minutes."

Sarah agreed to stay home and take care of the dogs while Audrey and I set out to help catch Blue Lady. Chief Sorensen offered to alert a patrolman in the area to call in any sightings. Then his own phone went off and he hurried out the door ahead of us.

Audrey tells me she's found a lot of lost dogs over her years with Redbud Area Dog Rescue. But she doesn't have a perfect record, and neither does anyone else.

"We have our share of sad stories – dogs that dart out a door and onto a busy street." She didn't need to say more. "We've had a few that disappeared never to be seen again. Sometimes that's the most heartbreaking of all. Not knowing what happened to the dog." Audrey told me about a few adopted dogs that had gotten away from their owners. The first few weeks in a new home are always the most risky. The dog hasn't yet bonded with its humans and is new to the new home and neighborhood.

Redbud Rescue does everything possible to help dogs find their way back home. We send them to their new homes with both microchips and tags. If the lost dog wags its way up to a friendly neighbor, that neighbor will either call the number on the tag or take the dog to a vet clinic or shelter to have it scanned for a microchip. The microchip is important because sometimes dogs lose their collars.

Audrey said microchip companies have stories of dogs being returned to their homes several years after going missing. The chips are injected into the skin between the shoulder blades. A scanner "reads" the number. A call to the microchip company can then link the number to the dog's owner.

Finding a frightened dog is more complicated. Scared dogs won't just walk up to someone with a dopey lost look in their eyes as if to say, "I'm not sure which way is home. Could you point the way, please?"

Scared dogs run from people, sometimes even from those they know and love. We were hoping Blue Lady would recognize me or Audrey and respond to our calls. But we weren't sure we would even spot her today. Blue Lady was a frightened dog still learning to trust people. I knew the odds were stacked against us getting her back.

Ira and his wife met us at the door, both wide-eyed and anxious. Ira had a stack of fliers in one hand. His wife Millie stepped outside to point off in the direction Blue Lady had run. We looked that way and then studied our surroundings. We noticed a few fortunate things right away. Ira and his wife lived in a house on a small lake. That meant a water source, something that would keep Blue Lady from wandering too far. Dogs will usually stay near a reliable water source as long as they can also find food and shelter as well.

Another fortunate thing we noticed was the absence of any busy street nearby. I felt a little more confident. Then several neighbors showed up while we were there, offering to help search. This was also a good sign. More eyes watching for Blue Lady.

The neighbors looked at Ira's flier with the picture of Blue Lady and the heading "Lost Pet." The rest of the flier gave a couple numbers to call and a line that said the dog was very frightened."

"Don't chase her. She'll run if she's scared," Audrey said. Then she grabbed some of the extra fliers and handed them around. "It's important to get these fliers to as many people as possible. Put them on posts too and at the closest gas stations and grocery stores.

"If you see her near your home, put out food. You might be able to lure her closer to you, maybe even into your yard or garage. Then you have a chance of trapping her where she can't get away from you."

Audrey barked out directions as if she'd given this lecture many times before, which I'm sure she had.

Next we climbed into the back seat of Ira's car and drove around the neighborhood. We stopped near the spot where he'd last seen Blue Lady. There we got out and walked towards a wooded area. "You might want to put some food out here. If she keeps coming back to the same place, we might be able to trap her."

We spent another couple hours driving around the neighborhood handing out fliers to everyone we saw and tucking some others inside storm doors. And everywhere, we watched for Blue Lady. Audrey had binoculars with her and would stand in one spot for several minutes slowly turning in a circle, binoculars scanning the horizons.

After we failed to spot Blue Lady, we left for home, suggesting Ira and Elizabeth leave food and water in both their front and back yards.

"Call me if you have any more sightings. If she stays in the same area, I'll bring out a humane trap and catch her that way."

On the way back, Audrey said she was a little optimistic. The neighbors are helping. That's good. And with water and food available, she won't need to go far."

"I hope you're right. I'd hate to lose that sweet dog after rescuing her at the auction. She was just beginning her new life." God how I hated all this losing business. I'd lost too much in my personal life. My dreams were about losing things. And now a lost dog, a precious lost dog. I needed to find something. I needed to find Blue Lady.

We pulled up to Audrey's home to see Sarah in the yard throwing a ball for a black lab, a white shepherd mix, and a blonde husky mix. She turned and waved. "Any luck?"

We shook our heads as we step on the porch.

Sarah came inside with her ball- chasing crew leaping around her. Then seeing Audrey and me, the dogs raced towards us.

"Don't let them jump on you," Audrey called. "Off. Off." We both braced ourselves and turned our backs on the dogs, nearly losing our balance with the happy welcoming assault. Finally we stooped down to accept their dog kisses. Audrey looked up at her daughter. "You looked like a mighty fine dog person out there."

"Not yet, mom. Not yet. Or should I saw MAAAHM?"

They both laughed.

Audrey looked my way. "If you don't mind, Judy, I'd like you to hold down the fort here while Sarah and I visit Bella's. Sarah's heading home tomorrow, so we need some quality mother/daughter time"

"My pleasure," I said.

Audrey hurried off to change out of her dog chasing ensemble. Sarah decided to go with what she was wearing – jeans and a pink cotton sweater.

A short time later, I watched them leave.

I'd forgotten to tell Audrey about the email from Lydia Harrison's daughter.

Chapter 40

After feeding all the dogs, cleaning up a little, and checking to see if Blue Lady was still missing, I sat down at the computer and opened the email from Lydia Harrison's daughter.

I'd met her only briefly while she was in Redbud arranging to bring her mother home. Lisa seemed as fragile as a bird and as fluttery. I guessed her as not quite 100 pounds and no taller than five feet. She whispered rather than talked and dressed as elegantly and as expensively as her mother. Her version of a hand shake was a soft touch on my palm.

I liked her. What can I say? Sometimes I meet someone and know right away that this is someone I'd enjoy knowing. We briefly spoke of our common ancestors and Lisa smiled sadly. "I wish she had never gotten so involved in genealogy. But that's my mom. Once she takes on a project, everyone needs to just stay out of her way."

I'd laughed politely. "I know what you mean. I'm a little that way myself."

During our conversation then, Lisa said she'd go through her mother's apartment in New York and would let us know if she learned anything that might be helpful to the murder investigation. As an afterthought, she'd added, "Or anything she might have learned about our Nebraska ancestors. Mother talked about her genealogical research all the time, but I'll admit that I didn't always listen."

I started reading her email and quickly learned something that changed everything.

Lisa jumped right in with the most startling news of all. She knew Audrey's sister. She also knew her nephew.

"I didn't make the connection until I got home and looked at mother's appointment books. Also, the woman and son my mother knew seemed very close. But Audrey told me that her sister was afraid of her son and had been hiding from him for many years. So yes, I am as confused as I know you must be."

I quickly scanned through the email and saw that Lydia and Jessica had worked together in the Twin Towers. They'd been work place friends but hadn't socialized outside of work. Several times the son had dropped by to go to lunch with his mother and Jessica had introduced him to Lydia. Also, somewhere along the line, the two women learned that their ancestors had settled in the same Nebraska town. I don't know if they had yet figured out that they had the same ancestors.

"I don't think mother knew Jessica all that well. They mainly just shared work and work place gossip. Then came 911 and Jessica and Lydia helped each other down the stairs and out the building.

"Mother later saw Jessica listed among the missing and wondered about that. We thought that maybe she'd gone back in looking for someone or something. It all seemed rather strange and sad."

Strange and sad indeed, I thought. As his mother's only survivor, Charles Nesbitt could have received a large settlement from the 911 commission. Jessica probably also had a large life insurance policy. So instead of walking away from 911 for her own safety, Jessica may have faked her own death so that she and her son could benefit financially. Why then had Jessica been telling Audrey even before 911 that she was afraid of Charles and needed to hide from him?

Maybe Jessica was planning to fake her own death some other way. Her son would collect the life insurance, and both of them would benefit. Then 911 made it easier and more lucrative.

As I read on, I saw that Lydia never went back to the stock brokerage where she and Jessica had worked. Instead she became involved with animal rescue and became the executive director and chief fundraiser for a New York animal shelter.

"I was there when Charles walked in pretending to be looking for a pet," Lisa wrote. "I was just a volunteer walking two little dogs through the lobby when I overheard him asking to talk to my mother. He said he was also interested in making a large donation.

"Naturally, mother stepped out and introduced herself. I noticed the way she looked at him and wondered if she already knew him. She told him he looked familiar and they finally figured it out. Then mother told him how she'd always wondered how Jessica ended up as one of the victims after the two of them had safely exited the South Tower together.

"We later wondered if he'd come to the shelter specifically to check her out or if their meeting there was just a coincidence. I remember his saying that his father, who was also deceased, had been a veterinarian. So maybe it made sense that he would want to help support an animal shelter. What didn't make sense is that he left without making a donation or adopting a dog. He didn't even look at the dogs.

"A few days later no other than Jessica herself walked in the shelter. Mother couldn't believe it."

Lisa wrote that Jessica said that in all the confusion after 911, her name ended up on the missing list. She said it was nearly impossible to convince anyone that she was still alive. But there she was. Quite alive.

"To say my mother was shocked would be putting it mildly. She also didn't believe a word Jessica told her, but she quickly realized that she'd better pretend she did."

Lisa wrote that Jessica continued to drop by the shelter "just to chat. By this time, mother was wondering if she should call the police or the FBI about Jessica and try to find out the truth. Jessica's frequent visits were beginning to worry her."

As I read on, I saw that Lydia was becoming more and more involved in researching her Nebraska roots. She'd found her grandmother's girlhood diary which had fired up her interest even more. She retired from the shelter and was planning her trip to Nebraska, thinking she'd live there awhile and maybe even stay if she liked it enough. Maybe she could even put her shelter experience to work in Redbud. As Lydia planned her trip to Nebraska, she still wondered what she should do about Jessica, who'd dropped out of view after Lydia's retirement from the dog shelter. Then one day she literally ran in to Jessica on the street outside her apartment.

"Mother told me Jessica acted all surprised to see her. Then mother made the mistake of saying she'd be visiting Redbud, Nebraska, soon to conduct more research into her family roots. Jessica said she had a sister in Redbud and had been meaning to visit there for a long time. Mother tried to keep secret her travel plans but somehow Jessica must have figured it out."

Lisa's email continued with the line, "I can only imagine what she thought when she saw Jessica in Nebraska." Then at the bottom, she added this note: "I attached a diary."

I could imagine what Audrey must have felt. Caution? Fear? Confusion? Any of those things. I remembered how Audrey said her sister could be very charming. And maybe disarming? Did Lydia invite Jessica to follow her to the house? Or couldn't she stop her?

I clicked on the attachment titled "diary" and picked up my phone to call Chief Sorensen. Lisa had copied him on the same email. What did he think? What would he do? But before I could finish dialing or read one word of the diary, the house phone rang. I grabbed that phone and heard an excited Ira saying three neighbors had spotted Blue Lady in the same area. One of them left some food out and had seen her return several times. When they walked towards her, however, she ran back into the wooded area. Could someone bring out a trap?

It was already dark and I didn't know much about setting up a trap, so I called Audrey for advice. She told me where to find the right trap and told me to call her again when I got out to the site. She'd walk me through the setup.

"Bring yummy, aromatic food. Anything a dog might find irresistible."

I put away the dogs, locked the house and lugged the trap out to my car. I could barely fit it into my car, even with the back seat reclined. At Ira's place, we transferred the trap to his truck and headed for the area where we would set up the trap.

With Audrey on the phone, we managed to set the trap properly so that Lady Blue (or any other hungry animal) could enter the trap, move toward the food at the far end, and step on a lever that would cause the door behind it to drop, trapping it safely inside. With everything in place, Ira drove me back to my car and promised he'd check the trap early the next day.

I drove towards Audrey's place, then braked and turned around. The night was chilly and the Nebraska sky especially dark. I returned to the road closest to the trap site and watched it with the windows down, waiting for the slightest whisper, the faintest movement.

After about 30 minutes in the car, I tiptoed to a spot on an incline just above the trap and sheltered under a tree with low-hanging branches. From here I would see if Lady Blue or any other animal approached the trap. A shadow crept across the moon and the night shuddered. I pulled my sweater tighter and tucked my head down. I didn't want to use the word "creepy," but I felt like I was in the company of spirits. Every shadow seemed alive and every sound suggested footsteps crunching through the grass. As the moment when I was ready to dash to my car, I heard the trap snap. At the same time, the shadow over the moon slipped off, and the night grew gently and lighter.

I breathed again and slid down the incline to the trap. Blue Lady peeked through the bars at me.

"You stay right there. I'm taking you home."

I called Ira who appeared in his truck within minutes. We lifted the trap onto the truck. I followed him home where we closed the truck in the garage and then coaxed the quivering Blue Lady out of the trap.

I think she was happy to see us.

Chapter 41

We found her! God Damn! We found her! Blue Lady is home safe!

I sang all the way home. Whatever was playing on the radio, I sang along happily, my hands thumping percussion on the steering wheel. We found her! She isn't lost anymore! Tonight maybe I'd dream about finding things instead of losing them!

The world was looking better. Leaving Ira's neighborhood, I turned on the road that would take me through downtown Redbud and then out into the country and on to Audrey's place. I sang my way past a dark Bella's and on down the main drag, noticing not a soul on the street to enjoy my trilling. Checking my phone, I saw it was almost out of juice – one lonely bar, barely enough to tell me the time – 1:35 a.m. Redbud is not a late night sort of town. I wondered if Audrey and Sarah were still up talking but didn't want to wake them if they were already in bed.

But still! We found her! Audrey had warned me that we might not find Blue Lady. We might not get a happy ending. Scared dogs are hard to catch. Sometimes a trap will catch them, but everything needs to work out just right for that.

And everything did work out right! We found the right spot, the right night, and the right food.

I sang on. I thumped away on the steering wheel. I couldn't remember the last time I'd felt this good. God Damn! We found Blue Lady! I hoped Audrey and Sarah would still be awake when I got home. I wanted to tell them right away

As I left the town limits, I noticed a pale car turn out of a side street and pull in behind me. I didn't pay much attention to it at first. Another late owl? A few minutes later I checked my rearview mirror and saw it still behind me, but not close anymore, hanging back a distance. I expected it to turn off somewhere between here and Audrey's. But what if it didn't pull off? What if it was following me?

Damn! With all the excitement about catching Blue Lady in the trap, I'd forgotten about the crunch of steps behind me as I sat under the tree's branches, the shadow of a man lunging towards me, his racing away as I screamed. No more singing. I slowed down. The car behind me maintained the same distance. I sped up. Same thing. The same distance.

I pulled into Audrey's driveway and saw lights within like bright square eyes. They were still up! I looked down the road but didn't see the car following me anymore. Maybe it had turned off somewhere. Silly me, I thought. I hurried out of the car and towards the house. Then I stopped and backed away. Audrey and Sarah were not alone. With them was another woman who could only be Audrey's sister, Jessica.

Audrey didn't know. I hadn't had time to tell her about the email from Lydia Harrison's daughter. I ducked around to the side of the house nearest the three women. What should I do? How could I warn them? I heard laughter inside as I slid down below the window and tried to hear what they were saying. This was what Audrey had wanted -- a chance to talk with her long-lost sister, a chance to set things right between them in spite of all their differences.

I pulled my phone out of my pocket to call Chef Sorensen. He didn't answer and the phone died before I could leave a message. With the little juice left in my phone, I dialed 911 just as the screen went dark. Damn.

Leaning up against the outside wall, I could just barely follow the conversation inside. Audrey was saying something sympathetic about how difficult it must have been for Jessica hiding from her own son, never able to stay in one place for long or apply for a job with her own name. "How did you manage?"

Jessica just laughed.

"And how did you get away from him? Where is he now?"

Jessica laughed louder and then her tone changed.

"Are you so stupid, Audrey? Are you really that stupid?"

The room feel silent. I could imagine the expression on Audrey's face and on that of her daughter."

"I'm not afraid of Charles. I've never been afraid of Charles although he's been rightly afraid of me at times. We are a team – a good team. Did you really believe all the things I told you? Poor naïve Audrey. Poor stupid Audrey."

She spit out her words and I listened in silence, fingering my phone again, hoping my 911 call would go through.

Ugly. Ugly. Ugly. I threw my phone into the grass.

"Do you want the truth? The whole truth? Of course, Charles is a killer. He's been a killer since he was 14. The time when he was accused of killing a classmate? I helped him. I showed him how. I told him that he can't let people walk all over him. I helped him cover it up too."

I thought I heard Audrey gasp. Carefully, I pulled myself up just high enough to see in the window. Jessica's back was towards me, but Audrey briefly caught my eye as Jessica pulled something out of her purse. A Gun. Sarah leaned against her mother and covered her hand with one of her own.

"Like this gun?" She waved it from Audrey to Sarah. "Wine is so much nicer, but we both figured you'd be careful about accepting a glass of wine from anyone now – even me or maybe especially me. So I guess I need to try something different."

"Why?"

Jessica laughed again. "Oh, Audrey. Why? Maybe just because you thought you could boss me around when we were children. And you'd be doing it still if I let you."

"You're killing people because I was a bossy big sister?"

"*We've* been killing people. Understand that? *We've* been killing people. Charles and I. We made a pact to never let anyone boss us around anymore. His wife was bossy. We killed her and everyone thought it was suicide." She laughed again. The brilliant part was the way I actually accused Charles of murder. I knew what I was doing. He knew what I was doing. It was brilliant."

"Then when I was planning to fake my death so that Charles could collect my large insurance payout, the most wonderful thing happened. Two planes crashed into the Twin Towers. Opportunity. Not only did Charles collect my insurance payout, he also received compensation because of my death in the Twin Towers."

Oh no. This woman is really insane. What can I do? I sunk my head into my hands. Did Chief Sorensen get my message? Where is he?

"But why kill Dog Ladies?" Audrey sounded calm. I knew she wasn't.

"That came later. Before then we killed a couple men just for money. They were men I'd married with one of my phony names. They both enjoyed a glass of wine before bed. Imagine that.

"And then, of course, along came Lydia Harrison. I knew she might turn me in. I don't think she believed my story about the newspaper making a mistake. I tried to charm her. I acted interested in her research into her ancestors, who I think are also our ancestors. Right, Audrey? That's when I found out about all the money that was hidden out here. Money you knew about, Audrey." By now Jessica was on her feet, towering over Audrey and Sarah, waving the gun.

"First you took the man I wanted. And now you're taking money and not sharing it with me."

I thought I heard Audrey laugh, a sad laugh. "Oh Jessica."

And then she asked again. "But why kill Dog Ladies?"

"They're all so bossy too. I wanted a puppy. I tried to adopt one, and the woman in charge of the rescue group turned me down. I told her the puppy would have a nice dog house but that dogs didn't belong in the house. I wouldn't hear of that. And she turned me down. So I sent Charles to kill her. He brought her a lost dog and told her he was a wine salesman. When she accepted the lost dog, he insisted on giving her an expensive bottle of wine. He even poured the glass for her. Wine doused with phenobarbital. Good night. He enjoyed it. He enjoyed watching her die.

"Then it just seemed like such a good path to you, Audrey. Year after year, I keep thinking about you. I envied you. You seemed more content than I ever was. I thought when I killed your husband that you might become bitter. Did you know I killed him? I killed Charles' father too."

"And now I'm going to kill you and your lovely daughter."

Where was Chief Sorensen? Where were the other police? I had to do something. I looked around frantically, finally finding a large rock which I hurled at the window.

I heard the crashing of glass, the screams, the gunshots, the sirens, the stomping of a thousand horses, the hissing of a voice in my ear as an arm wrapped around my nick. Then the pain. Then darkness.

Chapter 42

Am I dreaming? Am I alive? Through a fog, I hear mumbling, shouting, then nothing. I slip back into another world. My old word, the one I don't want to revisit.

I'm late for work. Paul and I are both gulping down coffee. "Honey, please. Can you drop the baby off at the sitter's today? I have an early interview."

"Uh huh. OK," he murmurs. I'm in a sleeveless dress, appropriate for the scorching July day, but I'll need the matching jacket I'm carrying over one arm. The air conditioning in the office is always a little too low for me.

"Thanks. I owe you." I kiss him on the cheek. The baby is already in his car seat which is on the kitchen table. With purse and jacket draped over one arm, I scoop up the baby in his car seat. Paul opens the door for me, and I shuffle into the garage.

I'm muttering to myself about nothing in particular as I toss purse and jacket into my front seat. Then I open the back seat of Paul's car and begin fastening car seat and baby in securely, facing backwards. I lean in to kiss my sleeping boy on his forehead. "See you tonight."

I'm backing out of the driveway as Paul steps into the garage. I wave. He waves back and opens the front door of his car.

Mornings are such a rush.

It all starts over again. I'm late for work. I have an early interview. I ask Paul to drop off the baby at the sitters. He agrees. I leave. I fasten the baby and car seat into his back seat. I leave. He leaves.

Again and again in my mind, my dream, my former world, I circle back to those few minutes. And then as if finally breaking loose, my memories move forward.

I've just returned from interviewing a man who had announced his candidacy for mayor. As I walk into the newsroom, an assistant city editor waves at me frantically.

"What's up?"

"Your baby sitter's on the phone."

I'd turned off my cellphone during the interview, so my babysitter must have called the news room.

"Is something wrong?" I ask the sitter.

"I don't know. He's not here. Wasn't he coming today?"

I drop the phone. I feel the sweat under my arms staining my dress. I look straight into the glaring sunlight out the window.

I dialed. "Where is he? Tell me he's with you."

Then he says the words that changed my life forever.

"I forgot. I forgot I had him. Oh no. Oh God. Oh no."

I ran from the office and drove to Paul's office, horn blasting at every car that blocked my speed. I pulled into his parking lot in time to see the ambulance next to Paul's car. Paul was sitting on the ground next to his car, his hands covering his eyes. A policeman was crouched next to him with an arm across Paul's shoulders.

I knew.

I knew.

I screamed. Did I scream then or was I screaming now? I heard the voices again, anxious and sharp. "I think she's walking up." But then I wasn't. I was back in my nightmare.

"Is he alive? Is he alive?" At the door to the ambulance, someone stopped me. He doesn't need to say more. I turned to the hunched form of my husband, stepped towards him, leaned down and pulled his hands away from his tear-stained face. "How could you forget? How could you? You killed our baby. You killed our baby."

I remember his eyes, hollow and absent. He said nothing.

Later I would learn that 30 to 40 babies died every year after being left in a hot car. I'd heard of such things, but I'd always thought the parents must have been terrible people who stopped for a cold drink somewhere and left their babies to die from the heat. I learned that more than half of the deaths involved people like us. The person with the baby simple forgot the baby was in the car. I was usually the one dropping off the baby at the sitters. Paul was tired. Maybe he didn't even remember agreeing to take the baby. The police tried to tell us this was something that could happen to anyone. But we couldn't agree.

174

I remembered the newspaper article about our baby's death. It was as if it was in front of my eyes, reminding me. The article advised people to do something to remind themselves that the baby was in the back seat. Leave your left shoe in the backseat...or your purse or briefcase. Anything that will force you to look in the back seat. The article tells me that deaths of infants in hot cars went up after front seat air bags became mandatory. Parents no longer had their babies in the front seat with them.

None of that helped us. We buried our babies, and two weeks later Paul ran off the road and smashed into a telephone pole.

I felt myself sobbing. My checks were wet.

"I think she's coming around."

I opened my eyes to three unfamiliar faces leaning over me. And one familiar one. Audrey.

I closed my eyes and went back to sleep.

Audrey was alive. They hadn't killed her. But what was wrong with me. Where was I?

I felt someone shaking my shoulder.

"Judy. You need to wake up."

"Don't want to."

I heard a couple chuckles.

"Judy!"

I opened my eyes again. I hurt. My head hurt. My stomach hurt. I tried to focus on the other faces.

"Where am I?"

"You're in the hospital, Judy. Do you remember what happened?"

I scrunched up my face. I remembered heaving a rock through a window, trying to distract Jessica so she wouldn't shoot Audrey and Sarah.

"I remember the sound of gun shots. I remember someone grabbing me from behind. Pain. Then nothing."

A man I assumed was a doctor shone a light into one eye, then another. "You had surgery four days ago. We were wondering when you'd come back to us."

"I heard shots. Was I shot?

"Shot and stabbed. You lost a lot of blood. We weren't sure you'd survive, but half of Redbud showed up to donate blood."

Audrey now pushed aside the doctor. "When you pitched the rock through the window, Jessica turned and shot at you. She grazed one side of your head. You're going to need some sort of bonnet for a while. But it was Charles who did the real damage. Chief Sorensen said he'd been following you. When he saw you crouched outside the window, he crept just close enough to see what you were doing. When he saw you with the rock, he rushed towards you with a hunting knife. Oh Judy, he barely missed your heart."

I touched the bandages covering my midsection.

"Is Sarah ok?"

"Yes. Just fine. She was one of those who gave blood. She's back in California now but calls me almost every hour to see how you're doing.

"I heard sirens."

"When you threw the rock and Jessica turned to shoot you, the police were already running from their patrol cars. Chief Sorensen got suspicious when he couldn't reach me. He'd read the email from Lydia Harrison and knew we were in trouble. He'd also spotted Charles earlier in the day and was keeping him under surveillance. While Charles was tracking you, the Chief was not far behind.

"My eyelids fluttered. Staying awake was hard."

"What about Jessica and Charles?"

"Charles is in custody, claiming he was helplessly under his mother's control."

"And Jessica"

Audrey looked at her feet. "Everything happened so fast. Jessica was facing the window as a couple police officers came through the front door with guns out. She turned towards them with gun extended. Both officers fired."

"She's dead."

"Yes. Oh Judy. I'm so sorry. I feel so guilty. My own sister. We didn't have a perfect childhood, but why? I don't understand how she could have done the things she did."

"Sometimes it just happens that way." I don't know how those words ended up in my mouth. Weren't they from one of my dreams?

The doctor suggested that everyone leave and let me rest.

I closed my eyes. The last words I remembered were from Audrey saying something about a diary.

Chapter 43

I stayed in the hospital a few more days. On one of those days I talked to Audrey about my husband and baby and everything that had happened. She'd known my story all along, probably from the day I arrived, but I thought it was time for me to talk about it out loud. Another day I told my story to Bella and Carl, who more than anyone else understood why I'd needed to stay silent for so long. Then I talked to Lois and Barbara, who both cried. Finally, I talked to Chief Sorensen.

Did I feel better after talking about losing my baby and then my husband? I'm not really sure of that, but it was time to talk. My secret past, even if it wasn't so secret, was like something caught in my throat. Releasing it helped me breathe. For too long, I'd floated above those memories, not even allowing them into my dreams except for sudden flashes my subconscious quickly rejected. I felt the loss but tried to forget those I had lost.

They deserve my memory. I will never forget them. I will talk about them now from time to time now. I will take out the photograph of the three of us and set it in plain view. But I will not walk into every room with sadness on both arms. My feet are on the ground. I have survived.

A few years before I lost what I thought was my entire world, I'd interviewed a psychiatrist about holocaust survivors. I said something about how amazing it was that people could survive so much intact. He was silent for a while, thoughtful. "They can survive, but not always intact."

I don't pretend to compare myself to holocaust survivors. I survived my own tragedy, but I'm not the same. Pieces of what I used to be have fallen away. Some things are harder for me now – and some things are easier. I'm not intact. I'm not the same.

But I'm going to be fine. I know that now. Redbud and the people I've met here have helped heal me. And let's not forget the dogs. They've helped, can I say, the most of all? Did they rescue me? Maybe I've turned into a dog person after all. I remembered how Audrey would always tell me not to worry about my dreams, not to worry about being happy, but just take care of the dogs. It's all about dogs, she said. Maybe she's right.

And then there's the matter of my ancestors. I guess I'll never know the whole story about Karen and Johannes. But the stories Lars Sorensen and I pieced together – those stories feel right or at least right in all the important ways. Karen was someone who ran from her own past and found a new life in Nebraska. That's something we share. She also tragically lost a child in circumstances that must have left her feeling guilty, must have left both Karen and Johannes feeling responsible.

I'll never live down the angry words I hurled at Paul, the way I blamed him for killing our baby. Part of me will always feel responsible for both their deaths. I imagine that such thoughts tormented Karen at times too. But she lived on and so will I.

I wonder what Karen and Johannes would think if they knew about all their ancestors? The good and the bad. Audrey and Jessica. Carl. Lydia. Charles. Me. And so many others. I once read that if you trace your ancestors back far enough you'll find both kings and paupers, saints and sinners. I'm sure the same rule applies to descendants.

Sometimes, though, I think about all the family stories and wonder if they aren't the work of an overly active imagination or of someone who prefers a grandiose embellishment to a less interesting truth. Was the real truth about Karen that she never told the truth? Or was that the real truth about Johannes?

Chapter 44

On my last day in the hospital, Chief Sorensen (who now says "Call me Randy," but I still have trouble doing it) showed up with a gift. I ripped off the paper which looked like something left over from a couple Christmases ago and pulled out two knitted hats.

"Just what I wanted," I said with all honesty. "More than that, just what I needed." I patted the shorn left side of my head. The first hat was lightweight and of various shades of purple and rose, perfect for fall. I pulled it on my head and liked the way it covered everything and curled back up slightly along the edges.

"You'll need the other before you know it," he said.

"I picked up the grey wool cap and admired the ear flaps." Oh dear. I wasn't ready to even think about winter.

"And I'm almost done with a matching scarf."

"Tell me, please. How did this happen? You've got to be the only police chief in the world who knits."

He picked up the wool cap and turned it around in his hands. "Knitting helped me quit drinking."

Audrey had told me he had a history of alcoholism, a habit that had cost him a marriage and almost a career. I knew he was strictly a soft drink man now.

"Does AA know about this? It could help others." I had a sudden vision of AA meetings where it would be hard to hear any speakers over the clicking of knitting needles. Every meeting would include time for an exchange of sweater patterns. Maybe knitting would become a new step.

He laughed. "Actually someone at an AA meeting suggested this to me. Then I found out that keeping both hands busy kept me from too easily picking up a drink. Knitting is a real stress reducer for me."

"But you're so...so good at it." I held up the light-weight hat and studied the pattern.

"Ahh shucks." He did a good job of acting embarrassed. Then he added, "The more complicated the pattern the easier it is to keep your mind off your own difficulties. And almost nothing beats the feeling that comes when you finish a difficult knitting project and know you got it right. It's almost as energizing as catching a murderer."

A tap tap at the door alerted us to Audrey's arrival.

"I brought you a change of clothes." She waved a package. "A new pair of jeans and a bright red t-shirt with the Redbud Area Dog Rescue logo on it."

"Who would want anything more?" Chief Sorensen remarked.

"Randy!" Audrey noticed him sitting by my bed. She spotted his latest knitting projects and hurried over to check them out. "You do such good work."

Then Audrey clapped her hands. "It's going home day. They're kicking you out of this place, Judy. Get changed and we'll all stop off at Bella's. Carl and Bella are expecting us."

A half hour later, we pulled up in from of Bella's. Carl and Bella met us at the door and I ended up in the center of a group hug. Funny thing is I doubt any of us were natural huggers being more from the stiff upper lip tradition. But hug we did. Circumstances called for it.

"Wait till you see what we found in the diary," Carl chimed as he pulled me towards a corner table.

I sat down to see a pile of printed pages in from of me with the title "Hannah Jensen's Diary." As I thumbed through the pages, I saw a number of passages circled with yellow marker. Maybe this would solve some of the mysteries of our family stories.

I looked across the table at Carl and smiled. "So are we all going to be rich?" He shrugged and straightened his mustache with one hand. He pointed at the top page in front of me.

I read out loud. *"Today I sat on the lap of the Queen of Denmark. Can you believe that, Diary? I can't. Mama said she'd come to visit Danes now living in America. She also said the queen was sort of a distant relative. Mama says a lot of things like that, though, and papa always laughs and says something like "Don't get all carried away again, Karen." Then mama would give him a mean look but only one mean look. Then she'd smile at him.*

"The Queen of Denmark and a few others with her stopped at our house to say hello. Mama and all of us had cleaned for two weeks all day

long to make sure everything sparkled. Then mama led them in and grandly opened the pocket doors to the dining room where she'd laid out tea and little treats. The visitors nibbled mama's treats and sipped tea. Then the queen sat down and I stood right next to her. That's how she happened to pat her lap and ask me if I'd like to sit there for a while. I did. She had on the longest pearl necklace I'd ever seen. She let me play with it while I sat on her lap.

When finally they left, the Queen pulled the necklace over her head and handed it to mama, who tried to give it back. The Queen insisted mama keep it!"

Wow! So the Queen of Denmark visited Redbud and gave our ancestor a long pearl necklace. I wonder what happened to it.

"Read on." Carl moved aside some of the top pages and pointed at another circled passage.

Audrey and Randy (hard not to say Chief Sorensen) both sat back in their chairs with arms crossed, waiting for me to finish reading the diary's circled parts. Bella was back and forth from the kitchen with trays of finger foods.

So I read on.

"My big sister Carrie says gambling is evil. She says all card playing is evil. She didn't used to feel that way. She used to play cards with papa, mama, Jens, Emily and sometimes Mary. Carrie was a good player, too. Almost as good as papa."

I looked up. My grandmother said something about card playing. "She said they used to play cards a lot and were good at it, but they always closed the curtain so no one would see what they were doing."

Randy (Chief Sorensen) interrupted. "There was a period in Redbud history when many of the immigrant Danes were divided into two groups. People would talk about the Good Time Danes and the Sober Danes. It was really about a theological divide in the Danish Lutheran Church, with the so-called Sober Danes asking people to look inward for answers and not to search for fulfillment in outside pursuits. They found a lot of those outside pursuits unworthy and usually sinful. I'm just guessing here, but the Sober Danes probably didn't think much of gambling or gamblers." He chuckled as he pulled some yarn and knitting needles out of a bag by his chair. I saw the same color as my new winter cap. My scarf!

After taking a closer look at the scarf that would be keeping me warm in a few months, I looked back at the diary and read out loud again.

"Carrie started it. She pulled back her long curly hair into a plain bun because she said it was wrong to call attention to her hair which was bright and beautiful. Then she stomped out into the yard and walked towards the corn field. When she came back, she said she'd pulled off the diamond earrings papa gave her for her birthday and had hurled them into the field. She said papa paid for them with his gambling money and that made the earrings just as evil as the gambling.

Papa stayed out of her way, hoping she'd get tired of all the new religious stuff. But it didn't happen that way. In the end, Carrie talked Emily and Mary and finally mama into going to the new church. Then they all started working on papa. He finally gave in and we were soon all proper church goers at a church where even loud singing brought warning glances from the pastor."

I looked up and smiled.

"Go on. Go on." Carl gestured with his hands as if shooing something away.

Bella slipped into the chair next to Carl. "You're just getting to the good part."

I turned over a few pages until I came to another circled section. I cleared my throat and began reading.

"I heard mama and poppa whispering together in the kitchen one night. They didn't know I was awake and sitting on the stairs. Papa was willing to quit gambling, but he said he wasn't going to throw away or give away his gambling money. He said we might need it someday. "What if someone gets sick? What if I get sick and can't work the farm? What if we have a couple bad crops in a row?' Mama said something I couldn't hear. Then papa said, 'Leave it to me. I'll hide it where no one will think of knowing.' Then I heard mama say, 'What about the necklace?' I knew she meant the necklace from the Queen of Denmark. Papa said he had a special place for that."

"So where did he hide it all? And how much did he hide?" I looked up from my reading at all the faces. Carl could no longer wait for me to go on reading. He clapped his hands together. "I think we'll be finding out tomorrow."

Carl quickly summarized what he'd read in the diary. Johannes had hidden bags full of coins in various hiding spots in the house. He'd also hidden some inside the chairs he was so fond of making. Besides that, he buried a few boxes around the farm. Our little diary writer was also quite the sleuth. She shadowed her father while he found safe hiding places for his gold coins and for the pearl necklace.

But didn't they ever need the money? Didn't they run into any bad times when money was short? Those thoughts ran through my head. What made us think there was anything yet to find? For that matter, what made us think that gamblers always won? Maybe Johannes snuck off for one last night of gambling and lost it all? And if Johannes didn't lose it all or need it all to meet expenses on the farm, wouldn't some of the readers of the diary have conducted their own successful treasure hunt long ago? I expressed my concerns out loud.

Chief Sorensen looked up from his knitting. "When Lydia Harrison started contacting me about her Redbud ancestors, she said she'd just found a diary that her grandmother had left her. She'd been cleaning out some boxes left in storage when she dusted off the diary. She didn't remember ever seeing it before."

So, I thought. The diary was hidden away in a box for all those years. Then Lydia finds it and decides to learn more about her ancestors and maybe even go on a treasure hunt. But what about Jessica? Had Lydia mentioned something about the diary to Jessica while they were both working in the same office? Had the diary been the main reason Jessica decided to drop in on Lydia at the animal shelter? The reason she and Charles followed Lydia to Nebraska?

Audrey seemed to read my thoughts. "Maybe Jessica was running low on cash, or maybe she just wanted more. She got Charles involved and they managed to arrive in Redbud the same day Lydia left Bella's to move into the old Jensen farm house."

"Do we know what happened at the farm house?" I ask Chief Sorensen this question. He nods.

"Charles told us Jessica started off friendly, asking Lydia if she'd let her look at the diary. When Lydia said she didn't have the diary with her, Jessica became suspicious and then hostile. She accused Lydia of all sorts of crimes and insisted that they should all share any treasures they might find. Finally Lydia agreed to share and told them a little about what was in the diary."

I remembered the yawning hole in the kitchen wall, the chunks of drywall, the dust and debris.

"Did they find anything?"

"Charles said they didn't, but I'm not sure I believe him. Would you? Maybe they did and decided to celebrate with a glass of wine – wine they'd brought with them. My guess is that they grabbed the coins they'd found inside the kitchen wall and took off as soon as they saw the phenobarbital doing its job on Lydia."

I imagined the scene. Lydia realizing that something was terribly wrong, staggering after Jessica and Charles and finally collapsing halfway out the door, one arm reaching out for help.

"Then what?"

Audrey and Randy filled in the rest with a combination of facts and speculation. Jessica and Charles planned to return but decided to wait until someone discovered Lydia and the authorities deemed it a suicide. They hoped that's what would happen. If anyone did catch up with them, they were going to say they'd left much earlier and that they didn't know anything about the destruction in the kitchen or what Lydia might have done after they left. Unfortunately for them, they were careless, leaving fingerprints behind on their wine glasses.

I'm surprised they were that careless. No one found fingerprints at any of the other Dog Lady murder sites."

Chief Sorensen thought about that only a few seconds. "No one was looking for fingerprints initially when the cases all looked like suicide. But I suspect something happened at Lydia's and they didn't take time to wipe away their prints. Or maybe they thought it would be even more suspicious if they did wipe away their prints. They had a story that might have worked. Jessica had run into Lydia at Bella's. Lydia had invited her to see the farm house. Charles told us they were prepared to say that they saw someone driving up to the house as they left. They also considered saying Lydia seemed depressed when they didn't find any treasures inside the kitchen wall.

I added. "And maybe Jessica had another plan – one she didn't share with Charles. She would blame it all on Charles, if necessary, even saying he'd kidnapped her. Jessica was ready to give up Charles if that would save her."

But things didn't turn out that way for Jessica. And Charles wasted no time turning on his mother. What a family, I thought, and then remembered they were Audrey's family and distantly my own. How could two daughters from the same family turn out so differently? And yet I knew from my own newspaper experience that things like that happened all the time. Good parents would sometimes see a son or daughter turn into a monster. I'd seen bewildered parent sitting in the courtroom as their child went on trial for murder. What would be worse, I sometimes wondered, to be the parent of a murdered child or the parent of a child who murdered?

Audrey had said she and Jessica didn't have a perfect childhood. I resolved to learn more about Audrey in the months ahead but knew it might be difficult. Audrey didn't share her secrets easily.

But why all the other Dog Lady murders?"

Everyone looked at me with what looked like a universal shrug.

Carl jumped in now with a little of his own speculation. "I guess she didn't know about me. She didn't want to share anything she found with anyone – not even her sister. So she decided to get Audrey out of the way."

The Chief added: "And we know Jessica held a lifelong grudge against Audrey, holding her responsible for everything that might have gone wrong in her life. I also think Jessica was starting to fall apart. Years of living a lie, of living 'off the grid,' of hiding from one crime after another was taking its toll on her. Somehow it made sense to her that she would mow a path to Audrey by killing off some of other Dog Ladies."

I remembered the conversation I'd overheard while huddled outside Audrey's living room window.

Well it didn't make sense to me or to any of the others sitting around our table.

"So what next?"

Carl reached beside his chair and pulled up his metal detector.

"Tomorrow we all go on a treasure hunt. We have the map there." He pointed at the papers in front of me. He hesitated. "Do you feel up to it, Judy? We can always bring along a lawn chair and you can supervise."

I said I'd be fine, but I had a couple more questions.

"Why do we think we'll find anything? Why didn't Johannes and his family need it long ago? Or why didn't someone else find it all by now?"

Carl pointed at the papers again. He said that our little diary writer didn't say much about the hidden money until late in the diary when she wrote about her father's death and noted that he kept his promise about never gambling again. She also said the family never needed the hidden treasures and when she left home to attend college, she decided to just leave the hidden coins and necklace where they rested. She didn't need them and she didn't want to see her sisters and brothers fighting over them

Hmm. I mentioned that Johannes did leave his children enough money in his will so that each of them could buy a new home. Where did that come from?

Carl winked. "He might have put some money away many years before the religious revival. Or he might have lived frugally and set aside money every month like we're all supposed to do but usually don't. And we still don't know if Karen's family might have left her some money. That's another possibility for the money in the will."

My final question was this? "What if we actually find something?"

Chapter 45

I woke up alone in my bed. I'd decided it was best if I didn't have several dogs poking me and bouncing around near me just yet, so I'd closed the door to keep them out. I'd slept well – no dreams that I remembered. But I woke up reaching out for a dog to pet and found none. That seemed wrong, and I sighed.

Last night I'd met Buster, a feral dog who could climb a 6-foot-fence but who kept climbing back over it to eat and live with us, sneaking slightly closer to us every day. He still backed away whenever we stepped towards him. He still raced across the yard and over the fence if anything frightened him, such as a new car pulling into the driveway. He still wouldn't let us touch him. But he looked at us more, and he usually kept us in sight. He was a 40 pound black and tan shepherd mix with soulful brown eyes. Audrey said he'd come to us from a hoarding situation. Animal control had finally trapped him and asked if we'd give him a chance. They even delivered him to us so that they wouldn't need to remove him from his crate until he was safely inside our fence. That was before we learned that the fence wouldn't hold him.

And yet he'd decided to stay with us. He followed the other dogs around and seemed content. We knew, though, that he could take off any time the spirit moved him.

Audrey said he hadn't progressed much in the days he'd been with Redbud Area Dog Rescue, but that the fact that he didn't leave seemed promising. My hope was that eventually he'd find his way onto my bed.

I heard Audrey clattering about in the kitchen and carefully pulled myself into a sitting position. As I stepped into the kitchen to say good morning, Audrey shooed me back to my room. "Rest some more. I've got everything covered here. I'm ordering you back to bed for a couple hours. Then we'll get ready for our crazy treasure hunt." She shook her head. "I still don't really think we'll find anything, but Carl is all fired up."

I happily turned around and headed back to bed.

Two hours later Audrey woke me. I dressed in my new jeans and t-shirt. Audrey tossed me an extra sweatshirt in case the weather cooled. We grabbed a couple folding lawn chairs and tromped out to the van. Before we left, we gave each of the crated dogs a biscuit. "We won't be gone long boys and girls." Audrey sounded optimistic. I wasn't so sure.

Carl was waiting out front. He reported that Bella had stayed behind to take care of the lunch crowd but might join us later. Chief Sorensen had dropped off the keys but was too busy with police work to stay.

Where do we begin?" I stepped inside and looked around. Every corner appeared in my mind to be hiding something valuable.

Carl's suggestion was that we check the kitchen first, paying attending most to the gaping hole in the wall. "Maybe they missed something."

Carl stepped up to the hole and began moving his metal detector across all the surfaces outside and inside the hole. Finally he slowly waved the detector across the flooring inside the hole. Nothing.

"If there was anything here, Jessica and Charles found it." He turned into the living room and stared at the fireplace, saying there was supposed to be a hollow place behind one of the bricks. Audrey and I began pulling at the individual bricks while Carl tapped along the wall beside the fireplace listening for hollow places. We were about to move on when Audrey wiggled a brick near the bottom and yelped as it came loose. She slowly pulled the brick out and then reached inside and after moving her arm about and scrunching her face into a frown, she finally pulled her arm back out with her hand clasped around a red velvet bag. She opened it, turned it over and shook out a long pearl necklace.

I gasped. "It's true!"

I picked the necklace off the floor and ran it through my fingers. "I wonder if it's the real thing."

"We can always find that out." Audrey took it from me and looked it over. Thank goodness she didn't try rubbing it against her teeth. I've always doubted that little test. Instead, she said, "We'll take it to a jeweler. Real or not, it sure is beautiful. I thought of a small girl sitting on the lap of the Queen of Denmark, finger the pearls as she gazed into the face of the beautiful lady smiling back at her.

I marveled that as old as the house was, it will still standing and hiding its secrets. As if reading my mind, Carl said the fireplace was part of the original house, but that much of the home had been added or replaced over time. Then he said we needed to check out the basement.

Chief Sorensen and I had discovered a nearly hidden room in the basement. I remembered him admiring an old chair there, rocking it back and forth and commenting on the weight. After a few minutes in the room, we knew why the chair seemed so heavy. Carl's metal detector woke up with a fury of ticks as Carl passed it near the chair. Aha! He pulled a pocket knife from a back pocket and slashed open the back of the chair. Two bags fell to the floor and several dozen gold coins spilled out and rolled across the floor. Audrey and I shrieked and fell to our knees, scooping up the coins and returning them to the bags. Carl was speechless. When he could finally catch his breath enough to talk, he said that each of those coins was probably worth several hundred dollars. A few might be worth in the thousands.

"They're worth a lot more now than the numbers on their faces. That's for sure."

And that's for sure nothing Johannes would have imagined when he hid them inside the chair for safekeeping. We then turned to the other two chairs in the room, and found more piles of gold coins.

"Where next?" I asked. I wondered if this was the last of what we'd find in the house.

Carl looked to his notes. "It says he hid something in every chair he made, but some of those chairs are probably long gone."

"We saw some chairs in the barn." I remembered the time Chief Sorensen and I had looked around the property.

And so we marched out to the barn, Carl in the lead with Audrey following close behind him and with me trailed them slowly while pressing my hands to my still-bandaged midsection. By the time I caught up, Carl had already ripped open one of the chairs. Audrey was pouring out a golden stream of coins. I gasped. Two chairs later we knew we had a small fortune, maybe a large fortune in old gold coins. We all sat on the dusty floor as Carl started picking up the coins one by one and exclaiming about what he read on their faces.

Next we tried to locate several burial spots the diary had mentioned. With those efforts, we failed. Someone really must have dug up at least some of the coins. Maybe Johannes and his family did have some bad years.

What do we do now? We all wondered the same thing, I was sure. Can we claim the coins after all these years? Is it all a case of 'finder's keepers'? Did they all belong to the property owner, which we knew to be Chief Sorensen?

"I never really believed the stories." Audrey held one coin close to her eyes and turned it over in her hand. She said nothing for several minutes as she picked up and examined several more coins. "Lydia Harrison's daughter needs to be part of this. It was the diary she found that brought us to this moment."

Audrey didn't seem to find this moment all that happy. I understood her mood. So did Carl. We tried to remain solemn, but it was so hard not to inject a little joy and excitement into the moment. But Audrey must have been remembering that her sister Jessica, along with her son Charles, had killed several people at least in part because of their lust for these coins.

"We'll find a way to make things right. These coins and the necklace can inspire good as well as evil," I said.

We all agreed.

Chapter 46

The necklace was a fake.

Did anyone really believe the Queen of Denmark would have handed over the genuine article to a farmer's wife in Nebraska? She probably traveled with dozens of faux pearl necklaces, leaving the genuine ones at home in a safe.

But the coins were real and worth an incredible $5 million. Stories of the discovered coins made headlines across the country and throughout the Internet. As a result, several hundred people claimed the coins belonged to them.

Carl, Audrey, Chief Sorensen, Lydia Harrison's daughter, and I all met to decide what to do with the $5 million. If you are thinking we fought bitterly and parted as enemies, you'd be wrong. We all agreed the money should serve some good purpose.

We weren't total angels, however. Each of us took $100,000 for our individual enjoyment and security. That left us with $4.5 million. Our next step was to purchase the property from Chief Sorensen to use as a second location for Redbud Area Dog Rescue. The Chief made that easier and less expensive by offering to donate the property. With that settled, we designated $50,000 for fencing, a new kennel, and other repairs and updates on the property.

With the remaining funds, we decided to set up a foundation. One purpose of the foundation would be to provide college scholarships to people who were descended from early settlers in the Redbud area. The Chief, as the local historian, already had a lengthy list of people who'd contacted him about ancestors in the area. We'd start with that list.

The foundation's other purpose would be to provide funding for low-cost spay/neuter programs and help with emergency veterinary expenses for dogs of persons who otherwise might not be able to afford treatment.

Satisfied with our plan, we shook hands and went about individual projects. For Audrey and I that meant preparing for yet another adoption event and for visiting one of our local shelters. We stopped first at the shelter and brought home a handsome collie mix we named Moritz. He played in the yard happily and steadily until he finally collapsed exhausted on one of our dog beds. Some dogs are so excited about their freedom that they can't stop themselves from testing their legs and their lungs for as long as they can.

Moritz has a special talent which should help him find a home. When he stands on his back legs, he can wrap his front legs around you in a fuzzy-dog hug. Add in a few dog kisses.

The same week we took in Moritz, we adopted out six dogs at a Saturday adoption event. One of them was Coco, the one I'd blogged about. A young woman showed up asking for Coco and saying she'd read about her in my blog. It was love at first sight. Coco liked Maryanne, and Maryanne quickly pronounced Coco "beautiful."

That same day we found homes for two other hard-to-adopt dogs – one a chubby senior black lab named Ellie Mae. The other a grey-faced rat terrier mix named Montana. Conventional wisdom would have kept those two with us forever. But then conventional wisdom is often wrong, I've found.

Conventional wisdom would say that I should return to St. Louis and resume my previous career or at least find a "real" job. But as winter crept closer and I pulled on my wool cap with the ear flaps, I hesitated and spent a lot of time studying the sky, often now a metal grey I should have found frightening but no longer did. I spent one afternoon walking about my ancestor's farm and sitting for long stretches on the bench by the lake. If the lake froze over, would I learn to ice skate? Audrey suggested I might want to move into the property since Redbud Area Dog Rescue now owned it. I'd only be responsible for utilities, taxes and insurance. Could I do it? Could I be happy here?

I knew I could live for quite a while without a real job. I had most of the savings I'd acquired from my life in St. Louis and now the additional $100,000. But eventually I'd need some sort of career beyond just caring for dogs. Redbud Rescue didn't have the funds to pay anyone salaries, not even Audrey. Maybe I could become a rookie police officer and work for Chief Sorensen. Ha! Maybe I could find a newspaper job. But with what's happening with newspapers now, I knew I couldn't count on that. Could I pick up enough freelance writing and editing?

Finally I decided not to decide just yet. I'd stay at least until spring and then decide on my next move.

Audrey was still a mystery I wanted to solve. How could I leave without knowing more about her past and the paths that led her to Redbud? And would I ever find a better café/meeting spot than Bella's? Shoot, maybe I could learn to cook. I could work there. What about Lois and Barbara and all the other volunteers and dog foster parents? I barely knew most of them, and I did want to know them better.

One day I visited Ira to see how Blue Lady was getting along. She was still shy but I smiled at the way she hid behind Ira as I walked into the living room. She was home to stay, I could see. I wondered too what might have happened if I hadn't been out watching the trap we'd set out for Blue Lady that night. How odd that I'd returned home in such a high ecstatic mood only to end up shot, stabbed and nearly killed.

But I lived. Since that night, Redbud had gone back to being a quiet, sleepy town where nothing much ever happened – or so the young folks said. Chief Sorensen dropped by quite often, and I noticed the comfortable way he and Audrey laughed and talked. He was teaching her to knit, and she always had a lot of questions for him. Maybe that was the purpose for all their phone calls? How could I leave without knowing how that turned out?

Fern and Thistle went in for their first heartworm treatment. I couldn't leave Redbud before they were done with treatment and healthy again.

One day Audrey and I cleared out the Redbud Rescue van and drove to St. Louis to empty out my storage compartment. I'd squirreled away a few pieces of furniture I thought I might want some day along with some scrapbooks of old photos I thought I'd never want to look through again. But now I wanted them too.

I'd forgotten about the chair I'd inherited from my mother which she had inherited from her mother. Somehow I'd always found a spot for it. And there it was, a chair just like the others that had poured forth all the golden coins. Audrey and I looked at each other. We loaded the chair into the van and left the search for later.

Once home we called Carl, Bella, and Randy (Chief Sorensen) to join us as we cut through the chair's upholstery. We first cut into the bottom of the chair.

Nothing fell out.

We tried the back of the chair.

Nothing fell out.

We tried the seat.

Nothing fell out.

Finally Carl looked at the two knobs that seemed part of the design carved onto the frame at the top. He twisted the knob and it came off in his hand. I reached in and pulled out a pair of earrings.

"I guess she didn't throw them out into the field." I remembered the story about how my great grandmother had thrown her diamond earrings into the field because she had decided they were sinful.

Audrey smiled. "I think you should keep those. Maybe it's a sign that you should stay in Redbud."

Maybe it is.

I stayed through the winter and did buy ice skates. I wrapped my weak ankles and moved slowly around the pond, pushing one foot ahead and then the other. In time I developed slightly more grace and speed. Slightly more.

Throughout the winter we continued to rescue more dogs and take them to adoption events every nice weekend. I found out dogs hate rain but love snow. There is no more delightful sight than a pack of dogs playing in the snow.

By February, Buster the feral dog was sleeping at the foot of my bed. He still scaled the 6 –foot-fence whenever he pleased, but he spent most of his time now with his dog friends here. Sometimes he even lets us pet him.

I was beginning to think of myself as a dog person.

One early spring day, Audrey grabbed me by the arm and practically dragged me outside.

"Look!" She pointed at the line of trees I'd basically ignored until now. But now they were in bloom.

"They are always the first to blossom in the spring. I always think of them as a heartfelt apology for winter."

We both stood gazing at the Redbud trees. "I happily accept your apology," I whispered.

And in that moment I decided to stay.

Note to readers

This story is fiction, but all the dogs are real. When I'm not writing, I am the founder and president of the St. Louis Senior Dog Project, a dog rescue organization specializing in older dogs. We've rescued a lot of dogs, but we've never been involved in a murder mystery of our own and hope never to be a part of one. Some of the dog rescue scenes in *Redbud* are drawn from my own experiences, but I've taken a few liberties here and there.

You can visit the St. Louis Senior Dog Project website at www.stlsdp.org, our Facebook page at www.Facebook.com/St.LouisSeniorDogProject or my blog at www.seniordogproject.typepad.com. You can email me at EllenE9466@aol.com.

If you enjoyed *Redbud,* I hope you'll write a review and tell others about this book.

There is no such place as Redbud, Nebraska, but if you know of a town that makes you think of Redbud, please tell me about it.

All of the humans in this book are fiction. I made them up. Don't even try to figure out if they might be people you know. They aren't.

As for Karen and Johannes, I made up their stories too. It's true I have ancestors who settled in Nebraska in the 1870s, but they left behind no diaries and no answers to the questions I may have about my ancestors.

I am now working on another Dog Lady Mystery.